THE NAKED BATTLE

Lucilla now knew that her life had been empty before she came to Ecuador.

At home in England, she was little more than a maid for her beautiful, temperamental older sister. But here in Ecuador, life was one glorious adventure after another—beginning with her rescue of a handsome Spanish officer.

Now the fate of Simón Bolívar's entire rebel army was in Lucilla's hands—as well as the life of the man she loved.

BARBARA CARTLAND

Bantam Books by Barbara Cartland
Ask your bookseller for the books you have missed

Barbara Cartland's Library of Love

Barbara Cartland
The Naked Battle

BANTAM BOOKS
TORONTO · NEW YORK · LONDON

THE NAKED BATTLE
A Bantam Book / October 1977

ISBN 0–553–11410–7

Published simultaneously in the United States and Canada

Bantam Books are published by Bantam Books, Inc. Its trade-
mark consisting of the words "Bantam Books" and the por-
trayal of a bantam, is registered in the United States Patent
Office and in other countries. Marca Registrada. Bantam
Books, Inc. 666 Fifth Avenue, New York, New York 10019.

PRINTED IN THE UNITED STATES OF AMERICA

Author's Note

Manuela Sáenz won her battle with Simón Bolívar and she was the great and final love of his life.

One of the more brilliant Leaders of all time, the Liberator of a Continent, a man who sacrificed his wealth and his health in the service of the people, Simón Bolívar died of tuberculosis at forty-six, exiled and penniless in the house of one of his enemies.

It was not until twelve years after his death that Bolívar was raised in the hearts of the people to the glorious position that Manuela had always known would be his. But in her case there was no sympathy or forgiving.

The woman whose love had become a faith, who had sustained and inspired him, died of diphtheria, in absolute poverty, and all mention of her was expunged from Simón Bolívar's life story.

The truth was saved by Daniel O'Leary. It is to him that we owe the true story of this beautiful, remarkable, and controversial character.

He alone saw the hundreds of ardent, passionate letters written to her by her famous lover, which were burnt with her belongings after her death, and only a scrap of one remains:

I cannot live without you. I can see you
always, even though I am away from you.
Come! Come to me! Come now!

Chapter One

1822

Lucilla looked across the garden at the hills surrounding Quito and saw between their rounded tops a glimpse, through the clouds, of the white peaks of the High Andes.

It was not surprising, she thought, that this was often called the Enchanted Cloud City of Ecuador, as every moment she was here she found it more beautiful than the last.

They had sailed from England into the harbour of Guayaquil to learn with consternation that a battle had taken place and the Spaniards had been defeated.

Lucilla's father, Sir John Cunningham, could hardly believe the news was true.

He had come out from England in a ship filled with muskets and other fire-arms to sell to the Spaniards, and now it looked as if his journey had been in vain.

But he told himself optimistically that doubtless the rumours were inaccurate or exaggerated, and they had set off from the port towards Quito.

Lucilla was certainly not impressed by Guayaquil despite learning that the great harbour, forty miles long and three times as wide, was not only one of the best in South America but also had great historical associations.

All she saw were the houses of split bamboo raised on stilts lining streets that were quagmires; three

1

centuries of ravage by pirates and termites had left it
a tropical pest-hole, unsightly, unsanitary, and dangerous.

Her father was interested only in the ships anchored off the shore, some of which had been built in
Guayaquil itself, carrying the cocoa, cotton, and rubber
that poured out to the world and had given Ecuador
the reputation of being a treasure-house for commerce.

The Inn in which they had a badly cooked, unap-
petising meal before the carriages were ready was
squalid, dirty, and uncomfortable.

But Lucilla was not prepared to criticise; she was
only too thankful to have reached South America and
not to have been left at home.

Her sister, Catherine, however, had a great deal
to say, and had thrown one of her inevitable tantrums
when she did not get what she wanted. The first stage
of their journey was spent with Lucilla trying to soothe
her down.

She was only too willing to do anything for Catherine, seeing that it was entirely due to her that she
had been brought on a voyage which she had felt sure
would end in El Dorado.

In all his previous transactions with the Spaniards, Sir John Cunningham had sailed alone, but this
year he had been annoyed because he and Catherine
had not received an invitation he expected to a Ball
being given for the King at Devonshire House.

"Dammit all!" he exclaimed when he found they
had been overlooked. "This country is going to the
dogs! And who should be surprised, seeing that the
Monarch is always in debt and spends his time flirting
with fat old women instead of attending to affairs of
State!"

Neither Catherine nor Lucilla saw fit to answer
this outburst. Then Sir John exclaimed:

"All I can say is thank God I am going back to
South America! The Spaniards know how to treat a
gentleman like myself, and the last time I was in Lima
the Viceroy afforded me special privileges which I
deeply appreciated."

As he spoke, his eyes rested on his elder daughter, and some detached part of his mind, which was not incensed at the moment, realised how attractive she was.

There was no doubt that Catherine was beautiful.

She was in fact the image of what every man thought was a typical English beauty.

Her hair was golden, her eyes were vividly blue, and she had a pink-and-white complexion that made everyone who saw her compare her to a rose.

Suddenly, startlingly, Sir John had hit the table with his clenched fist.

"I will not stay here being treated in an off-hand manner by those who think themselves our betters!" he bellowed. "I will take you with me to Lima, Catherine. You will be a sensation there and the Spaniards will show you how true gentlemen behave to the women they admire."

"To Lima, Papa?" Catherine asked in astonishment.

"You heard what I said," Sir John replied. "Be ready to sail in a week. Bring your best clothes. If you think the ladies of Lima are out of touch with fashion, you are very much mistaken."

There was a note in his voice which told Lucilla, who was very perceptive, that the ladies of Lima had been to his liking. She had always known that since her mother died her father had been very much a "ladies' man."

From that moment on there was chaos—Catherine giving orders for new gowns, for bonnets, for mantels, for slippers, for gloves, for sun-shades, and for innumerable other things, with only Lucilla to procure them for her.

Lucilla had no time to think of herself; but even if she had she would have accepted the inevitable, that she would stay behind with Cousin Dorcas, who had lived in the house as a Chaperon since her mother's death and was half-crippled with arthritis and extremely disagreeable because of it.

Then, astonishingly, four days before they were due to sail, everything was changed.

Catherine had come late, as usual, into the

Dining-Room where her father and younger sister were breakfasting, to say with a stormy expression in her blue eyes:

"Hannah refuses to accompany me!"

"What do you mean—refuses?" Lucilla asked.

"You can hear, can you not?" Catherine asked rudely. "She says she is too old, and what is more, she is afraid of the sea."

"But Hannah has always looked after you," Lucilla exclaimed. "How are we to train anyone else in so short a time?"

She knew that this was almost impossible, seeing that Sir John, for all his riches, was not generous-handed when it came to paying servants, and anyway Catherine was a difficult mistress and the younger maids were afraid of her.

"I will talk to Hannah," she said aloud, rising from her place at the table.

"It is no use," Catherine replied angrily. "I have begged her, raged at her, and even offered her more money, but she is as obstinate as a mule. Unless we take her aboard forcibly, she will not come."

"Well, there is Rose," Lucilla suggested gently.

"She is cork-brained!" Catherine retorted. "Besides, she cannot sew."

"Emily is too young," Lucilla said, as if she were talking to herself. "Perhaps I had better go to the Domestic Bureau to see if there is anyone available."

"You had better come yourself," Catherine said surlily. "You are better than any of those half-wits— and for that matter, better than Hannah when it comes to sewing."

Lucilla stared at her in astonishment. Then, to her incredulous surprise, her father said:

"Perhaps that is a good idea! If I rent a house, as I intend to do, Lucilla can be my housekeeper. She knows the foods I like, and some of the Peruvian dishes are too hot for my stomach."

Lucilla stared at him.

"Do you really mean that, Papa?" she asked in a low voice.

"Of course I mean it!" Sir John said testily, and

because he always avoided domestic troubles he left the room.

Only when the ship finally left Portsmouth and was moving over the rough water of the Channel did Lucilla convince herself that she was not dreaming.

Always in the past she had been left behind, and, unless it was completely unavoidable, she was never included in any Ball, party, or entertainment to which her father took Catherine.

She had been quite young when she realised that he hated her and the mere sight of her irritated him, and humbly she told herself she could understand the reason.

It was not only that she was not beautiful or spectacular like Catherine. It was also because he had so desperately wanted a son, and a second daughter had not only been a bitter disappointment, but it was the last child his wife was able to give him.

Sir John Cunningham came from an ancient Scottish family.

There had been Cunninghams living in the Lowlands of Scotland for generations, who had farmed their land and been content in their ancient Castles, having no ambition to see the world.

John Cunningham had been different.

He was fired with an ambition to be rich, to travel, and to be of consequence.

The acquirement of wealth came easily to him, and when his father died and he inherited the Baronetcy he was determined to be of importance in the Social World which centred in London round the Regent and Carlton House.

But somehow he was never accepted as a friend or confidant of the man who had been acclaimed as "the First Gentleman in Europe."

There were plenty of hostesses who, because he was rich, welcomed Sir John to their Soirées, their Assemblies, and their Receptions, but he knew, as Catherine did, that they could not enter the "inner circle."

They were not accepted by those who considered themselves the very cream of London Society.

It was for that reason as well as for the fact that

he made money by them, Lucilla realised, that he enjoyed his trips abroad.

As a nobleman and as an Englishman he was acclaimed and entertained in the manner which he believed was his right but which was not accorded him in his own country.

He concentrated all his efforts on providing the Spaniards with the weapons they so urgently required and for which they were prepared to pay generously.

It was a blow that he had not anticipated that the Revolution which had been taking place in the eastern countries of South America should have reached Ecuador and Peru.

It was all, he knew, due to a General Simón Bolívar, who called himself "the Liberator," and who had been born into just the sort of Social World into which Sir John Cunningham would like to have been born himself.

Immensely rich, a descendant of an ancient family of great wealth and nobility, Bolívar was a Marquis in his own right.

Wildly attractive to women, with deep-set black eyes that were lively and penetrating, he was by the age of seventeen already adept in the ways of Eros.

He visited Paris, and then went to Spain to finish his education at the Royal Military Academy. Although he had an olive skin, it was said by the gossips that he had replaced Manuel de Godoy as Queen Louisa's lover.

He married, but his wife died of yellow fever, and Simón Bolívar settled down in Paris where he was attracted as if by mesmerism to Napoleon Bonaparte, who became his ideal.

Sir John heard the story and told it to his daughters that the man who changed Bolívar's life was the great scientist Alexander von Humboldt, who had returned from five years of travel in South America to have his books published in the French Capital.

He had met young Bolívar at a Salon and naturally talked of Spanish America.

"In truth what a brilliant fate is that of the New

World," Bolívar had remarked, "if only its people were free of their yoke."

"I believe your country is ready for its independence," Humboldt had answered, "but I cannot yet see the man who is to achieve it."

They were the words which started the Revolution.

Sir John Cunningham had been amused by the tales, which were repeated to him wherever he went, of what was happening in Venezuela and Colombia under Simón Bolívar's leadership.

Although he himself was prepared to accept whatever the Spaniards could pay him, it made him laugh to think that an Army which consisted mostly of ragamuffins, ill-armed and ill-equipped, had out-manoeuvred Spain's famous General Pablo Morillo and marched a thousand miles through the Andes to rout more Spaniards at Boyacá.

He also thought it quite a joke when he heard in 1819 that Bolívar had instigated the Union of Colombia, which was to include the former Viceroyalties of Venezuela, Columbia, and other countries when liberated.

"He has got guts, that young man!" Sir John Cunningham had said in his Clubs when Bolívar's successes were talked about and doubtless, he thought, exaggerated.

But he never anticipated that Bolívar would interfere with his business of taking Spanish gold in exchange for guns. Yet now he was told that Quito was in the hands of the Liberators. So what was he to do with his cargo?

He would have gone straight on to Lima, but he learnt to his consternation that a Patriot Army under General San Martín had taken over the city. The Spanish were mobilising outside, while inside, spies and *agents provocateurs* were attempting to undermine the new Republic.

Sir John Cunningham had therefore determined that he would visit Quito first and see for himself exactly what was happening.

After all, it might be merely a slight reverse, and privately he was quite convinced that the might of Imperial Spain would sweep back to power and the Patriots would be hanged, and drawn and quartered as they had been in the Revolution of 1809.

"Is it really safe to travel, Papa?" Catherine had asked nervously as they set off on excrutiating roads which fortunately were dry, so the wheels of their carriage instead of getting bogged down raised clouds of dust.

"We are English," Sir John answered. "We are safe wherever we go."

"I hope you are right," Catherine said petulantly. "I have no desire to end up dead on the roadside or find myself hanging from a tree."

Lucilla thought Catherine was being hysterical as she often was, but as they neared Quito the marks of battle were plain to see.

Houses were gutted, fields deserted, and, more sinister, having as they crossed the Atlantic read every book she could about the country she was to visit, Lucilla knew why there were so many condor birds about.

These great carrion-eating birds unfurled white muffs at their throats and rose into the air on giant wings as the carriage passed, leaving for a moment the rotting bodies they fed on.

Before the city came in sight there were to be seen stiff, dark figures hanging from the branches of mole trees, and nearer still, gibbets from which men hung by their necks, stiff and elongated.

'War is cruel, wicked, and terrible!' Lucilla thought to herself.

But she did not speak aloud, having no desire to make Catherine more apprehensive than she was already, and hoping that her father was right in believing in their invulnerability just because they were British.

Instead, she tried only to see the beauty of the land itself, the bare mountains flooded with sunshine, an occasional glimpse of distant peaks dazzlingly white with snow.

As soon as they reached Quito, Lucilla was to

realise what a vital part the mountains had played in the battle which had just taken place.

Because the people of Quito were friendly, garrulous, and excited, they told her over and over again what had happened.

It was only a small Patriot Army hastily flung together, but it had marched up the slopes of the Andes towards Quito, commanded by a brilliant young man whom Simón Bolívar had made a Field Marshal at the age of only twenty-eight.

José Sucre, with the wisdom and brilliance of a General far exceeding him in age, had deployed his forces for a frontal attack on Quito. Then he had moved the bulk of his troops on a cold, dark night up the side of the Pichincha Volcano, which hung over the city.

A dozen voices explained to Lucilla the astonishment and surprise of the Spanish Commander who had awakened to find the Patriots above him, and the Royalists had been forced to climb high up the mountain to give battle.

It had been an excitement and at the same time an entertainment that Quito had never experienced before.

Lucilla was told how the people climbed the roofs and the belfries of the Churches to get a glimpse of the battle that raged above them, half-hidden by the clouds.

"We did not know our fate," one lady said, "until we saw the Royalists in their blue and gold uniforms running down the sides of the mountains. Then we knew that Sucre had won and we were free!"

Tears came into her eyes as she spoke and Lucilla could realise how much it meant to the people who had been oppressed, subdued, and regimented against their will for centuries.

"They love their country," she told herself.

She learnt too that the people of Quito had loathed the Spaniards with a hatred that was perhaps more intense and more violent than that which was felt in any other country in South America.

Sir John had hastily adapted himself to the new conditions.

He had taken a house on the edge of the city that had been deserted hurriedly by the Spanish Vice-President who had scuttled away just in time to escape being taken prisoner or, like many of his compatriots, shot on sight.

There were a great many old scores to be paid off, old insults to be avenged, and it was not possible for Marshal Sucre to prevent a certain amount of unnecessary acts of revenge involving even torture.

It was not surprising, as people remembered vividly what had happened after the revolt of 1809 when the Revolution had failed and the Crown had won. Then the streets had swum with the blood of massacred Patriots.

The conspirators who were caught were hanged, while those of high rank were torn in pieces, their legs and arms tied to four horses which were driven off to different points of the compass.

Others were cut down from the hangman's noose while still alive and then were decapitated, and their heads were put in iron cages on display in the city.

Then their hearts were ripped from their bodies and thrown into a boiling cauldron in the centre of the plaza.

It was the President's order that these atrocities should be witnessed by the families of those condemned.

Lucilla could understand, after all the years of longing for revenge, the jubilation now that Quito was at last free.

But even so, when at night she heard a sudden scream as if the hiding-place of some Spaniard had been found, or a cry of elation from those who avenged themselves, she shivered.

After all, those who died or were tortured were people, people like herself; people who wanted to live without war, without cruelty, without misery.

It accentuated her feelings as she moved about the house to find the drawers of the chests filled with the clothes that had been left behind, jewels in a woman's dressing-table, and papers, orders, and documents left untidily on a desk.

She could not escape from the idea that she, her father, and her sister were interlopers peeping into someone's private life, intruding where they were not wanted.

Her father gave her orders to have everything that belonged to the departed Spaniards destroyed, but she disobeyed him and tidied the things away in cupboards which were not being used, locking the jewellery and intimate possessions in bottom drawers where they were not likely to be disturbed.

Every day she thought it would be hard to find a more beautiful house in the world. The huge court-yard with its fountain in the middle and the great stone pots containing bougainvillaea, geraniums, lilies, and roses were a delight to her eye, and she felt a thrill every time she entered it.

Round the galleries of the court-yard and in all the rooms there were pictures—pictures that had thrilled her as soon as she had time to look at them.

For the first few days this was impossible, because she had to engage servants, supervise the kitchen, and be permanently on call to Catherine.

"Press my dresses! Mend those laces! Where is my bonnet with the feathers? The slippers which go with my green gown? My sun-shade?"

Catherine might have been a General herself, the way she gave Lucilla orders, but that had always been her attitude towards her younger sister.

Fortunately Lucilla was used to coping with the household difficulties, for she had been more or less forced into the position of housekeeper ever since her mother's death.

She found it was quite easy to engage as many staff as her father was prepared to pay, and because wages were far lower than they were in London she soon had a number of competent servants looking after the house and also Catherine.

A girl who had been trained at the Convent could

do the sewing; another was an expert, Lucilla found, at laundering; a third could be taught to dress Catherine's hair in the latest fashions.

At last when Lucilla had a few moments to herself she had time to examine the pictures, realising that they were not only beautiful but unusual.

She had not then learnt that the paintings in Quito, like the carvings of the pulpits and the altars of the Church, had been executed by natives under the direction of the Church-building Priests.

But some of them were to be masters in the real sense of the word and their pictures were later to have a world-wide reputation.

All Lucilla knew at the moment was that they delighted her eyes and made her feel as if her senses were uplifted by their beauty so that they became part of herself and her soul.

At first she had felt a little dizzy and breathless in Quito because with the exception of La Paz it was the highest city in the world.

But she had soon become acclimatised to it and sometimes she felt as if the beauty of the dazzling snow-capped mountains under a sky the colour of lapis-lazuli made her feel as if her feet could no longer stay on the ground and she was floating disembodied amongst the clouds that hid innumerable other peaks.

Lucilla moved away reluctantly from a picture of a sweet-faced Madonna framed in a wreath of flowers of every shape and colour and turned from the court-yard into a room near the entrance hall.

She thought from the desk and various masculine-style leather-covered chairs that it must have been the office or private Study of the Vice-President.

Then she saw on the wall opposite the window a number of portraits all of Officers wearing the formal Royal uniform of white piped with gold, and skin-tight pantaloons which moulded the legs, braided with arabesques.

Medals, dress-swords, and highly polished boots made them look impressive, and at the same time almost unhuman, like puppets on a stage.

She stared at the portraits one after the other,

realising that the one in the central position was the President of Quito, General Aymerich, while the man in the portrait on the right was the Vice-President and owner of the house.

The portrait on the left was of a man who in some strange way held Lucilla's attention so that she could no longer look at the others.

He was, she thought, taller than the President, more broad-shouldered, dark-haired, with eyes that seemed cold and hard, even though the artist must have wished to flatter him.

He had a strong aquiline nose that was characteristic of the Spanish nobility; his mouth was firm, yet not cruel; and there was, although she could not explain it, a kind of reserve, an inner withdrawal, besides a pride in his bearing.

She did not know why he attracted her, because since she had come to Quito she had told herself that if half the stories she had heard about the Spaniards were true, the retribution they had suffered was thoroughly deserved.

But this man was different—or was he?

Perhaps, she told herself, he was more guilty than all the others because he looked not only well bred but also extremely intelligent.

He must have known, he must have understood, that the manner in which his people were treating the Indians was wrong, that the wealth they took from the country should have gone to those who lived there, and that his allegiance to Spain should have been tempered by a love also for South America.

"I am being ridiculous!" Lucilla said to herself. "Why should he feel like that?"

But her eyes went back to him again. There was something about him, something that drew her, although she did not understand it.

Then underneath the portrait she saw his name: *Don Carlos De Olañeta*

He was certainly Spanish, a nobleman, a soldier, a man who perhaps had been as cruel as the people of Quito told her all the *godos* had been—cruel to the point of bestiality.

"I do not believe it!" Lucilla said aloud.

Then because she did not understand herself and her own feelings, she went from the room, closing the door quietly behind her.

She knew she would go back; even as she walked away into the flower-filled court-yard and saw the sun iridescent on the water of the fountain springing towards the sky, she knew that she would go back and look at the portrait of that strange man whose face seemed already to be etched on her mind.

* * *

Catherine returned to the house later that afternoon flushed with excitement.

Have you heard the news?" she asked almost breathlessly.

"Heard what?" Lucilla enquired.

"General Bolívar is on his way here. He is coming to Quito! There is to be a great Reception! A Ball at the Larrea House, and we are all invited—even you!"

What Catherine had said was repeated and rere-peated until Lucilla began to think the name Bolívar would be written on her heart.

The whole city was determined to celebrate his victory and their freedom, and the usually placid, easy-going people were galvanised into action.

All day long, soldiers marched down the streets and out into the fields to train in close drill order.

Soldiers sat in doorways cleaning their muskets, or hung about the Squares and streets seeking the canteens which sold fermented corn beer, which left a strong sweet smell on the light air.

There were soldiers everywhere, and by order of their Commandant all the houses were freshly painted for the celebration of Liberation.

To Lucilla it was like seeing an artist upset a palette, as the one-storeyed houses of adobe began to look riotously raffish when tinted pink, or blue, or green, or carmine by chattering crowds of Indians who splashed the pigment over the walls with a reck-lessness which showed their excitement.

The whole city began to buzz in an undercurrent of fervour and excitement while there were still prisoners being mustered for a march to the sea.

Weary and glassy-eyed, they shuffled along escorted by guards flying the flags of the Republic of Gran Colombia.

The faces of the troops who had been captured were not Spanish, Lucilla saw; they were round, copper-coloured, and had the slanting Mongoloid eyes of Indians.

And the guards had Indian faces too. Uniformed in the ragged home-spun green piped with gold, they rode bare-foot, their feet in the shoe-shaped brass stirrups while their bare heels were festooned with huge rowelled spurs.

It all seemed strange, and even while she was glad the war was over and the Liberators had won, she could not help wondering how many of the prisoners would ever reach the sea, how many would die on the way.

Quito was no longer concerned with prisoners but only with preparing itself for the man whom already they were beginning to worship as though he were a god.

The people of Quito were a strange conglomeration of thirty thousand souls, of whom before the Revolution only six thousand were pure-blooded Spaniards.

Those of mixed blood, the *cholos,* numbered more than a third of the population, and they were the barbers, the store-keepers, the artisans, the factors, the scriveners, the carvers. They had been the knife-edge of the Revolution and had actively contributed to and worked for it.

The Indians were the bulk of the population. Dressed in knee-length cotton trousers and woollen *ponchos,* they were the farmers and labourers, who kept the wheels of the city turning even though they got no credit for it.

But for once, all, with the exception of the Spaniards, who had gone into hiding, were activated by one thought, one ambition: to welcome the man who had altered the face of South America—Simón Bolívar.

"Are you excited at the thought of meeting him?" Catherine asked her father two days before he was due in the city.

"I think he will be glad to see me," Sir John Cunningham said slowly.

Lucilla glanced at her father sharply.

"You intend to sell him your guns?"

"I am prepared to sell to whoever can pay me," Sir John answered complacently.

Lucilla wondered if it would be possible for General Bolívar to do so.

Already she had heard stories of how he had spent his own vast fortune on his wars; and the men in his Army had not been paid half of what they had been promised, and their weapons were in short supply.

If these stories were true, it was all the more incredible that Bolívar's forces had beaten the Spaniards, who had unlimited resources.

Lucilla knew that her father when it came to business was no sentimentalist and indeed had no generosity about him.

He had made his fortune by expecting cash on delivery and getting it.

She had a sudden fear that General Bolívar would not be able to meet her father's price, and the shipload of arms would go—where? Perhaps to the Spaniards.

They were not vanquished yet: there were stories that the Royalist Armies were forming again high up in the Andes and tales from Lima that the Spaniards were bringing down more stores from Panama.

Lucilla did not repeat to her father what she had heard. She only listened, and there was a great deal to listen to in Quito those days.

The following afternoon, despite every resolution not to do so, she went again to the room with the portraits.

She told herself during the night that what she

felt about the picture of Don Carlos de Olañeta was ridiculous. He was no different from the others. They were all proud, autocratic, cruel; they had no right in this country, but should go back to Spain, where they belonged.

But when she stood in front of the portrait there was the same magic, the same feeling of being drawn towards it.

She wished she could understand why. There was nothing sympathetic, kind, or gentle in Olañeta's face. He was handsome, but there was hardness in his eyes and sharp lines at his chin.

It was the face of a man who was prepared to be ruthless and was perhaps ambitious, and yet she still had that feeling that it did not show his whole self.

Something was hidden, something was kept back —but what? And why should it trouble her?

Resolutely she walked away and once again shut the door behind her.

She had the afternoon to herself.

The servants were fitting well into the routine she had mapped out for them. The young maids were keeping Catherine's clothes as she liked them, and Catherine herself was enjoying every moment of her visit to Quito.

There were parties almost every day in the houses of ladies who welcomed her because of her father's rank and because too she was a novelty, a foreigner, and therefore an attraction.

All the men-folk, as might be expected, found her entrancing.

Bouquets of flowers arrived every day and Catherine was already finding it hard to apportion her favours so that by encouraging one she did not give offence to another.

"What a success I am!" she had said to Lucilla last night as she changed to go out to dinner. "How right Papa was to bring me here. After all, among all those dark women I shine like a star."

She certainly looked beautiful in one of the new and elaborate gowns she had brought from London as, covered with a diaphanous wrap of blue the colour of her eyes, she set off with her father for a dinner which she assured Lucilla had been given almost entirely in her honour.

Lucilla never thought for one moment that it was strange that she had not been invited.

If she had been, Lucilla thought, Catherine or her father had refused on her behalf. Actually she had no wish to go with them, except that she wanted to meet the people of Quito.

It would be exciting, she felt, to know what they thought in this country that was so far away from her own and yet one of the most beautiful places she could imagine.

As if the beauty drew her, she went out into the garden which lay at the back of the house.

It was a riot of colour, the flowers growing in a lush profusion which spoke of the tropical sun.

Something in their straggling untidiness reminded Lucilla that she had not yet engaged a gardener.

It had slipped her mind because she had had so much to organise in the house. But she had learnt from Josefina, the oldest of the maids and the one she most trusted, that the previous gardener had been pressured by the Spaniards into the Army, and had either been killed or taken prisoner.

"Tomorrow I must find at least two men to start work," Lucilla reminded herself.

She decided as she went towards the end of the garden that there should be three gardeners.

There was much that needed doing and she had already found that the Indians worked spasmodically and were all too ready to take a *siesta* if no-one was watching them.

At the end of the garden there was a small Pavilion made of white stone like the house, but which had obviously not been painted for some time.

It must originally, Lucilla thought as she moved towards it, have been intended to look like a Grecian Pavilion, but somehow it had a Spanish air which took away its classical perfection.

"I suppose it is a handy place in which to keep the garden implements," she told herself.

There was purple bougainvillaea growing over one side of the Pavilion and clematis on the other.

She walked up the two steps and saw that the door in front of her was badly in need of painting.

She wondered why the Spaniards had neglected this part of their estate, and, being curious, she pushed open the door.

It moved more easily than she had expected, then inside the square room of the Pavilion, which was devoid of furniture, she saw a man.

He was standing up as if he had risen at her approach and for a moment because she was frightened she could not see him clearly.

Then she saw that he was a soldier, a soldier wearing the blue and gold uniform of the Spaniards.

For a moment she felt as if it was hard to breathe, then she looked at him and knew she had seen him before.

Incredibly, unbelievably, he was the man in the picture—Don Carlos de Olañeta!

She stared and as she did so she saw that blood was pouring down one side of his face from a gash in his forehead.

"You are wounded!" she exclaimed, and her voice seemed to echo back to her from the empty walls.

"No," he replied. "I am dead!"

As he spoke he slithered down onto the floor and lay still.

Chapter Two

Lucilla did not scream as another girl might have done, nor was she frightened.

She moved forward and knelt down beside the fallen man, putting her hand out to take his wrist and feel his pulse.

She noticed that both his hands were very dirty, as if he had been digging in the earth, perhaps making a hiding-place. His boots were dusty to the point where there was no polish on them.

But for the moment she was concerned only with his pulse, which was faint, very faint; but it was beating and he was therefore alive.

She would have liked to feel his heart but was too shy to undo the buttons of his tunic, and she knew that if she was to save his life she must have some help.

It was then that she realised that the breeches he wore were soaked with blood, and she thought he must have a wound on his thigh as well as the one on his forehead.

She rose to her feet, and leaving the Pavilion, shutting the door tightly behind her, she ran back to the house.

As she went she calculated what would be required: bandages, blankets, water, and a sponge to clean away the stains of blood which had run down his cheek.

Lucilla, through organising her father's houses both in London and in the country, was used to accidents: there was always someone in the household who was in trouble in one way or another.

Pantry-boys cut their hands when they were sharpening the knives; scullions slipped and fell on the flagged floors; house-maids burnt themselves on the smouldering cinders; there was hardly a week that she was not required to tend wounds or sores, abrasions or cuts.

But this was different, she knew, and she could not help wondering frantically if Don Carlos had been prophetic in saying that he was dead.

When she reached the house she knew there was only one person she could ask to help her, and that was Josefina.

The elderly woman was half-Spanish, half-Indian, and had an air of self-confidence about her which made Lucilla already feel that she could rely upon her.

There was no sign of anyone in the court-yard and she ran along the passage which led to the kitchen-quarters.

Here there was another court-yard, smaller and certainly not as beautiful, cluttered with all the things that the staff wanted to dry in the sun or had cleared out of the rooms they were using.

"Josefina!" Lucilla cried, and a moment later she heard the older woman's reply:

"Sí, Señorita."

She spoke in the soft, slurring voice that was characteristic of those who lived in Quito, and with the lisp in her Spanish that marked the speech of an Ecuadoran.

"Josefina, I want you!" Lucilla said as the elderly woman appeared, a white apron over her black dress, her face expressionless, with dark eyes which were obedient without being servile.

Lucilla drew her down the passage so that they were well out of earshot of the other servants.

"Josefina, someone is wounded and needs our help—a man. He is in the Pavilion in the garden."

Lucilla paused and looked at the woman and it seemed as if Josefina sensed that there was something more, something which Lucilla had not said.

Lucilla drew in her breath.

"He is a Spaniard. I know who he is. His portrait hangs in the room by the entrance."

She waited, then something made her say his name.

"He is, I know, Don Carlos de Olañeta!"

A strange expression crossed Josefina's face which Lucilla could not translate. It was only there for an instant, then it was gone.

"You say he is wounded, *Señorita?*"

"Yes, badly," Lucilla answered, "and because of it I cannot give him up to the authorities."

"No, *Señorita,* I understand."

"I have bandages which I was going to take to the Hospital. We shall also need water and blankets."

"I will see to it, *Señorita.*"

Josefina was moving away quickly down the passage before Lucilla had finished speaking, and now she ran to the Sitting-Room where there was a basket full of bandages which she had prepared for one of the servants to take to the Hospital.

All the ladies in Quito had been working in the Hospitals and the improvised buildings that were filled with wounded from the battle.

Lucilla meant to join them when she had time, but she had been too busy to leave the house.

Instead, learning that bandages were urgently needed, she had cut and rolled some in the evening while she sat with her father listening to what he had been doing during the day.

Now, she thought, they would come in useful, but they would be used for a man wearing a very different uniform.

There were of course some wounded Spaniards in the town, but from what she had heard, those who had not been killed either in battle or in the vengeance that followed were left to fend for themselves.

There were no attractive ladies to sit by their bedsides, and the doctors, already run off their feet, gave them perfunctory attention or none at all.

"No!" Lucilla said to herself. She would not send

Don Carlos to die from neglect even if he did not die of his wounds.

Besides, since he must have been a man of importance—otherwise his portrait would not be hanging on the wall beside the President's—there was every chance, if she handed him over to the Patriots, that they would execute him as cruelly as their fathers had been executed in the last Revolution.

As well as the bandages she placed in the basket a nightshirt of her father's and bottle of his best French brandy, which he had brought with him in the ship. Then she ran upstairs to take a pillow from one of the beds.

Josefina, she thought, could concern herself with the blankets. As she was leaving the bed-room she thought suddenly that perhaps the wounded man's clothes might have to be cut from him, and she put a pair of scissors into the basket.

She could not think of anything else, and ran downstairs again to find Josefina waiting for her by the garden-door, a pile of blankets in her arms—the thick warm woolly blankets that were so necessary at night and which were woven by the Indians from the wool of the sheep which roamed the mountains.

Lucilla opened the garden-door.

"We do not wish to be seen," she said, pausing for a moment.

"Only the best rooms overlook the garden, *Señorita*," Josefina replied.

That meant they were safe, for both Sir John and Catherine were out.

Lucilla wasted no more time but led the way through the flower-beds; as she did so, she wondered, with an anxiety that surprised her, whether when she reached the Pavilion she would find Don Carlos already dead.

He was lying on the floor where she had left him, but now there was a pool of blood at his side and the wound in his forehead was still bleeding.

She put down what she carried and knelt once again to feel his pulse.

"He is still alive!" she said, and heard the relief in her voice.

Then she looked at Josefina standing beside her.

"We must get him out of this uniform and hide it."

Josefina nodded.

"Sí, Señorita, and we need to have help, for he is a big man."

"Help?" Lucilla asked apprehensively.

"In the fields, *Señorita,* beyond the garden you will find Pedro. He is my brother. He is working among the potatoes."

She thought that Lucilla looked surprised, and she said hastily:

"He is not paid. I was going to ask you, *Señorita,* if you would employ him."

"We need a gardener," Lucilla replied.

"Pedro would be glad of employment, *Señorita,* but now we need his help here!"

Lucilla rose to her feet.

"It is wise to tell him who is here?" she asked.

"Pedro would betray no-one!" Josefina said firmly. "Hurry, *Señorita,* these wounds need attention."

Without arguing further, Lucilla ran from the Pavilion and saw that where the garden ended there was a large cultivated patch of ground covered with the purple flowers of the potato.

For a moment she thought there was no-one there, then she saw the wide hat and the woollen *poncho* of a man crouched down weeding at the far end of the ground.

She moved towards him, calling as she did so:

"Pedro! Pedro!"

He came towards her, an apprehensive expression on his face, and she guessed that he thought she would reprove him for working when he had not been engaged.

She spoke to him quickly in her fluent Spanish.

"Your sister, Josefina, wants you. We need your help, Pedro. She is in the little Pavilion."

For one moment he did not understand, obviously knowing it by a different name, but Lucilla pointed and he set off at once with the shuffling but rhythmic gait of an Indian who is used to carrying heavy loads on his back.

Lucilla followed him.

As she reached the Pavilion she heard Josefina giving orders in a low voice.

She came in through the door and Josefina looked up.

Lucilla could see she was already undressing Don Carlos.

"Leave this to us, *Señorita,*" she said. "It is not seemly for a young lady to see a naked man. We shall require a mattress. If you choose one that can be spared, then Pedro can fetch it."

She saw that Lucilla hesitated as if half-resenting the fact that she was being sent away.

"The *Señor* will also need food," Josefina said. "Ask Francisca for nourishing soup. If you tell her you are sending it to the Hospital she will believe you."

"Yes, of course," Lucilla said.

This was something she could do to help, and once again she ran to the house to give orders to Francisca, who was peeling onions in the kitchen.

"I have soup, good soup, *Señorita,*" she answered.

This was not surprising, for soup was one of the staple dishes of Ecuador.

As Lucilla knew, there was always a large stock-pot simmering on the stove filled with pieces of meat, cereal, potatoes, and cheese.

Francisca rose now to pour some of the soup into a large bowl.

It smelt fragrant and Lucilla knew it would taste delicious.

"Shall I send one of the girls to the Hospital with you, *Señorita?*"

"No, I intend to take it myself later," Lucilla answered.

"That is kind, *Señorita,* kind of an English lady to concern herself with our wounded."

"We must all help them to get well," Lucilla replied.

Francisca put a piece of clean linen over the bowl and tied it carefully round the edge with string.

"I think it would be nice," Lucilla said, "if I took a little food every day. Things that men who are really ill could eat. You are such a good cook, Francisca, I know they would appreciate your *luapingachos.*"

This was a mashed potato and cheese speciality which was served in nearly every house in Quito. Even her father found it easy to digest.

"I will make many, many dishes," Francisca said enthusiastically. "It is just that the *Señor* may not like to pay the bills."

"I will see to that," Lucilla said, "and I think, Francisca, it would be wise not to worry him by telling him what we are doing."

Francisca laughed.

"Never tell a man anything it if worries him, *Señorita.* What he does not know will not keep him awake at night."

"No, indeed," Lucilla agreed, "and this will be a secret between you and me."

"The wounded will bless you, *Señorita,*" Francisca said, and started to prepare the table for the food she would cook.

Carrying the soup carefully and remembering to collect some spoons from the Dining-Room as she passed it, Lucilla went back to the Pavilion.

By now Don Carlos had his head on a pillow and was covered with blankets.

Pedro rose from where he had been kneeling on the floor as Lucilla entered and said to him:

"There is a mattress on the bed in the small room on the left as you go up the stairs. Bring that here, but be careful that no-one sees you."

He hurried off and Lucilla set the soup down on the floor beside Josefina.

"I have told Francisca to cook some food every day for me to take to the Hospital," she said in a low voice.

"That was a clever idea, *Señorita*."

"Can we persuade him to eat?"

"I think first we will give him a little brandy," Josefina said. "His pulse is very weak. Perhaps he has been without food or any form of sustenance since the battle."

Lucilla thought that was likely, and between them they raised Don Carlos's head and spooned drop after drop of brandy between his lips.

At first it just trickled down his chin and it seemed as though it was impossible to make him swallow. Then at last as if the raw spirits hurt his mouth he turned his head from side to side as if to avoid what was being fed him.

Then involuntarily he swallowed what was already in his throat.

It took a few minutes but the brandy brought a little colour back to his face, his lips opened, and they gave him more.

"It will make his heart beat," Josefina said beneath her breath.

It was sometime later, after Pedro had returned with the mattress and they had laid it on the floor in the corner of the Pavilion and carefully lifted Don Carlos onto it, that he began to move and talk.

He was obviously delirious and it was hard to understand what he said, the words muttered and only half-enunciated.

"He will have a fever," Josefina said.

Lucilla personally thought he would be lucky if he did not develop pneumonia; he had doubtlesss been out at night, and while the days were very hot the nights were cold with an icy chill from the snows.

She had already heard how many soldiers had died in the High Andes and how Bolívar had lost a tenth of his Army before he left Colombia simply because of the conditions through which they had marched.

"Do you think he is warmer now?" she asked Josefina anxiously, as Don Carlos turned his head from side to side.

"Perhaps he is thirsty," Josefina answered, and they gave him some spoonfuls of soup.

"It is best for him not to have too much," Josefina said.

Lucilla gave a little sigh.

"I have a feeling we should go back to the house," she said, "but who will look after him?"

"Pedro will do that," Josefina answered. "He will stay with him all night."

"He will not be missed from where he lives?" Lucilla asked anxiously.

Josefina shook her head.

"Pedro is now your gardener, *Señorita*. It will be understandable that he would sleep near his work and he will allow no-one into this place."

Lucilla looked towards the pile of blood-stained clothes lying in a corner.

Josefina followed the direction of her eyes.

"Pedro will bury them," she said in a low voice.

Lucilla went to the door of the Pavilion.

Outside, Pedro was already working in the garden, tidying back the long strands of convolvulous.

She wanted to tell him how to look after the patient, but she knew it was getting late and if her father had returned he would wonder what had happened to her.

"Tell Pedro what to do, Josefina," she said.

She took one quick look back in the Pavilion and at Don Carlos lying on the mattress on the floor. He was now still, and for the moment she thought, because his eyes were shut, that he looked younger and less awe-inspiring than in his portrait in the house.

'How could I have known? How could I have guessed that this man of all others would need my help?' she thought.

Then because it seemed so strange and because the feeling the picture had evoked in her was hard to understand, she ran as swiftly as she could into the house.

*   *   *

The following day when she visited the Pavilion she thought that Don Carlos looked a little better.

Pedro reported that he had slept and although he had apparently not regained consciousness he had drunk a little of the soup and seemed so thirsty that he had given him some water as well.

Pedro was a quiet, humble little man who Lucilla thought was rather in awe of his sister, but at the same time he had a personality all his own.

He was clean and his hands were gentle and she was quite content to leave the man she thought of as her patient in his care.

It was not possible for her to stay in the Pavilion for more than a few minutes in the morning, but when Catherine had retired for her *siesta* she hurried through the garden, knowing that everyone would suppose that she too was resting in her room.

Josefina was placing on a tray the bowl which had contained one of Francisca's dishes which she had cooked for the wounded.

"The *Señor* has eaten a little," she told Lucilla with a note of triumph in her voice. "Now he will be stronger. Now, soon, the fever will begin to leave him."

"And his wounds?" Lucilla asked.

She knew that Josefina had deliberately bandaged the sabre-thrust in Don Carlos's thigh when she was not present.

When Lucilla had offered to help she merely said:

"It is not seemly, *Señorita*," and Lucilla was not prepared to argue with her.

Now Don Carlos had a bandage round his forehead which looked very white against the tan of his skin.

"Are the wounds healing?" Lucilla asked.

"They will," Josefina answered, "and this afternoon Pedro will get me some resin from a mulli tree, which is better than anything else."

Lucilla knew from her reading that the resin had been used by the Incas for the treatment of wounds.

It was still considered by the Indians of the Andes to be magical and that nothing the doctors could offer was anything like so effective.

Lucilla could only hope they were right, for as she had no way of obtaining any drugs or medicines without arousing suspicion, she knew that whether it was best or not for Don Carlos she had to trust in mulli.

She sat down on the floor for a little while, looking at the man lying on the mattress, and thinking, as she had thought before, that he had the most unusual face of any man she had ever seen before in her whole life.

She did not even know specifically what was so unusual about him: there was just something that aroused a strange feeling that she had never felt before except when she had looked at his portrait.

"He is a Spaniard, and I should hate him," she told herself.

At the same time, she knew she had been right, although she could not justify it, in instinctively wishing to save his life.

She dared not stay long, for Catherine needed her to supervise the fitting of a new gown that she would wear at the Victory Ball.

In fact when Lucilla returned to the house and went up to her bed-room Catherine said angrily:

"Where have you been? I have been calling for you. You know I want you to help me get the trimming of this gown right."

"I am sorry, Catherine," Lucilla said humbly.

"You know that it is important I should look smarter and more attractive than anyone else," Catherine said. "I even intend to vie with Manuela Sáenz, and Heaven knows that is going to be difficult since no-one talks of anyone else."

That was true, because next to General Bolívar, Manuela Sáenz was causing more excitement in Quito even than the tales of the battle.

Lucilla had already heard about her before she came to South America, because it was Manuela's husband, James Thorne, who had first introduced Sir John Cunningham to the Viceroy of Peru.

James Thorne, an Englishman and a ship-owner, Lucilla had learnt, came from Aylesbury, England, and according to Sir John he was a short, stocky man with grey eyes and was a devout Catholic.

"He is also a damned good businessman," Sir John said, "and we have a number of projects going which should make us both a great deal of money."

He had, however, on arrival at Guayaquil been annoyed to learn that James Thorne had gone to Panama, and instead of meeting him at Quito as expected there was only his wife, the beautiful Manuela, to take his place.

There were plenty of people to tell the Cunninghams about Manuela even though Sir John had known something about her before.

She had been born in Quito and was the illegitimate child of a Spanish nobleman.

He had been a member of the Town Council, the Captain of the King's Militia, and the Collector of the decimal tithes of the Kingdom of Quito.

According to what Sir John said, no-one had imagined that he had any interests outside his rich wife, his family, and his business of importing Spanish goods for the purpose of resale.

But the birth of his daughter Manuela by an eighteen-year-old Spanish girl had caused a scandal which had never been forgotten, and if she had been born to the sound of clacking tongues, Manuela in her turn had them chattering about her all her life.

At the age of seventeen she had been expelled from the Convent because she had run away with a young Spanish Officer.

Because Quito had grown too hot to hold her she had gone to Lima and there married James Thorne, a man much older than herself, and she became a familiar figure in the Highest Society of the city.

Now because her husband was away in Panama, Manuela had returned to her native land but in very different circumstances from the disgrace in which she had left it.

Although her husband had been a friend of the Royalists and intimate with the Viceroy, Manuela had secretly moved in the Revolutionary Circle that was conspiring against the Crown.

Her part in the conspiracies lost nothing in the telling, and Lucilla learnt, because people talked of little else, that she had run amazing risks.

Hidden under her *saya* and *manto,* the enveloping overgarments worn by the women of Lima, she had carried seditious proclamations from secret printing-presses to the Patriots, who pasted them at night all over the walls of the city.

When her husband found out about it he was furious.

As a foreigner he was supposed to be above local politics and as a businessman he abhorred any thought of revolution because it interfered with business.

But when the previous year General San Martín's Armies had moved into Lima to be pelted with rose-petals and confetti, Manuela had received her reward.

General San Martín had originated the Order of the Sun, a decoration and an honour rather like the *Légion d'Honneur,* which was awarded to 112 women, the outstanding Patriots of Lima who had risked their lives to help the Liberators.

It was, he said, "the badge of a new Republican Nobility, and undoubtedly the most coveted Order in the New World."

No wonder that Manuela, now returning to Quito, which she had left seven years earlier in disgrace, could hold her head high and face with bold eyes those who had criticised her.

She had come to call on Sir John soon after the Cunninghams had arrived, and, while he disapproved of her independence and even the part she had played in the Revolution, he could not help, because he was a man, being beguiled by her beauty while Lucilla had been fascinated by her.

Never had she thought that a woman could be so

lovely and at the same time look intensely and vividly alive.

Her oval face, her skin like alabaster, and her dark hair braided in heavy coils made her quite unlike any beauty Lucilla had ever seen before.

Her eyes were dark and challenging, and yet had a twinkle in them that was mischievous and sometimes mocking. Lucilla was not aware, although her father was, that her full lips were both sensitive and passionate, and it would be hard for any man, old or young, to resist her dazzling smile.

She had only stayed for a little while, but she seemed to leave an imprint on the atmosphere as if a bird of Paradise had flashed into the darkness of the house and set everything pulsating.

It was Manuela Sáenz, which was what everybody called her, although of course her married name was Thorne, who challenged Catherine's claim to being the greatest beauty in the city.

"I want General Bolívar to admire me," Catherine said, swinging the gauze skirt of her gown round her as she looked at herself in the long mirror. "I hear he is a wonderful dancer, Lucilla. I shall dance with him. Think of it, to dance with the Conqueror of South America! The man who has defeated the Spaniards!"

"Not completely," Lucilla said in a low voice. "I hear they still have large Armies gathering in the mountains, to overthrow General Bolívar and regain the power they have lost."

"The General will win, I am sure of it," Catherine retorted, "and anyway, when he arrives, we do not wish to speak of war and of battles, but of other, much more important things."

There was no need to ask what Catherine considered important. Her eyes were half-closed as she stared at herself in the mirror and her red lips were pouting provocatively.

Lucilla thought that it must be obvious that the General would admire her. Then insidiously the question came to her mind: What would Don Carlos think of her?

Her father had said often enough that the Spaniards loved beautiful women, and Catherine was very beautiful—there was no doubt about that.

As she stood choosing the trimmings for her gown, discarding first one lace, then another, trying lilies, then camelias with their flat green leaves as a further trimming, Lucilla thought no-one could be lovelier and at the same time more temperamental.

Perhaps Spaniards liked temperamental women and expected them to be difficult, but as far as she was concerned she found it very tiring.

Because something within her wanted to find fault with Catherine, she could not help saying:

"You should have some Spanish lessons while you are here. You mispronounced no less than three words in that last sentence."

"And if I did," Catherine asked carelessly, "does it matter? Most of the aristocrats can speak French and at least I can make myself understood."

Lucilla did not answer.

Her mother had been very insistent that both her daughters should learn languages.

Lucilla spoke French, Spanish, and a little Italian, but Catherine would never apply herself seriously to anything that had to do with learning.

She would start a book and throw it away when she was halfway through.

Even when she was a little girl there were a hundred other things she wished to do rather than study with a Governess.

She would play truant and go riding, join in games with her friends in the woods, or even hide in some inaccessible place simply because she could not be bothered to be taught.

Coming over in the ship Lucilla had been determined to make her Spanish more proficient than it was already.

She found another passenger, an elderly man, who was prepared to give her lessons.

She read every book in the ship's Library that was written in Spanish, and now she could not only understand but speak with proper idiom and correct grammar, which commanded the adoration of even the oldest and proudest families in Quito.

"People do not always bother to listen to what I have to say," Catherine said as if she followed Lucilla's thought. "They look at me, and that is enough."

There was undoubtedly some truth in this, Lucilla thought, for with the sun glinting on her golden hair and her skin very white against the camelias she had fixed to the bodice of her gown, she looked like a young goddess rising from the sea or moving as the Greeks might have seen her through the clouds which covered Mount Olympus.

"You really are very beautiful, Catherine!" Lucilla said honestly.

"I know," Catherine agreed. "Is it not fortunate?"

* * *

The days passed and the city was ready. It seemed as though the whole place was surging with an excitement which increased hourly like a tidal wave.

But Lucilla's thoughts were preoccupied only by the man who lay in the Pavilion.

There was no doubt that his body was growing stronger, but his mind was still lost and he was not conscious of anything that went on round him.

Sometimes he opened his eyes and stared unseeingly at the ceiling. At others he muttered and tossed, then muttered again, but made no sense in what he said.

"It is the wound in his forehead," Josefina said. "It was deep, and if we had been able to call a doctor perhaps he would have done something for him.

"Do you mean he will . . . always be like this?" Lucilla asked in a low voice.

"No, of course not, *Señorita,*" Josefina answered. "It is just that it will take time. The brain is a strange thing—a gift from God, and God can take it away."

Lucilla shivered and felt afraid.

Supposing Don Carlos never recovered normality? Supposing he remained as he was now, hovering, as it were, in a no-man's-land where no-one could reach him?

She would sit by his bed every afternoon, usually alone, while Josefina was busy with other things, and Pedro kept guard in the garden outside. Then she prayed.

She would pray that Don Carlos would be himself again.

She wanted to see him as he looked in the portrait, proud and imperious, looking at the world with hard, penetrating eyes as if he sought something he had not yet found.

Lucilla had gone back day after day to look at the portrait to see if it would tell her anything.

She did not know why, but she felt that it held a secret which could help the real man. But the picture could not speak and Don Carlos only murmured unintelligible words.

She had a feeling that he was fighting a battle within himself, though whether it was for survival or merely a memory of something he had sought before he was wounded, she could not guess.

All she knew was that as she sat beside him she felt only the God to whom she prayed could help him and otherwise they were powerless.

Josefina and Pedro shaved him every day, and his hands, which had been so dirty the first time she had touched them, were now clean.

He had long, thin fingers and square, filbert nails, hands that were sensitive, hands that were, she thought, those of a man who could be gentle.

She wished she knew more about him but dared not ask anyone.

What had he been like before the Revolution? He was obviously of importance, but she knew it would be unwise to ask questions about the Spaniards whom everyone hated. Besides, all the people wanted to talk about was Bolívar and Manuela.

"Manuela Sáenz is going to wear white," Catherine said poutingly. "I asked her, and she told me she has chosen it specially for the occasion. I must wear something different."

"But, Catherine, your gown is ready, and it is so beautiful. You could not look more attractive."

"I am not going to look like another edition of Manuela Sáenz," Catherine said angrily. "I want blue, pink, a green gown, anything rather than white! Otherwise how shall I stand out from the crowd?"

"You will stand out anyway," Lucilla said consolingly. "No-one will look as beautiful as you with your fair hair and blue eyes, Catherine. Surely you realise that?"

Catherine was unconvinced and Lucilla continued:

"They will notice your face, your hair—your gown will not really be important."

"I am not wearing white!" Catherine said sharply.

The dress-makers were brought back to the house and Lucilla stood for hours appraising first this material, then another, until she could have cried.

Finally it was really a triumph of Lucilla's diplomacy that Catherine agreed to wear the gown that had already been made, but she changed the camelias with which it was trimmed to pink roses.

It was actually extremely successful, the roses accentuating even better than the camelias the whiteness of Catherine's skin, the faint flush on her cheeks, the vivid blue of her eyes.

"No-one can miss seeing me now!" she said triumphantly when the gown was finished only a few hours before she was ready to wear it.

The sky was vivid with bursting rockets and high on Panecillo, the hill that dominated the centre of the city, cannons boomed and the thunder of the salute seemed to shake even the clouds hanging over the peaks.

All the Church bells were ringing in a clarion of exultation and the crowds in the street, jostling and fighting for a place of advantage, were being pushed back by the soldiers to clear the cobbled centre for the arrival of the Liberator.

Standing at the back of the balcony of Juan de Larrea's house, which was the finest in Quito, Lucilla looked down and thought she had never seen such a strange throng or so much confusion.

Even after days of feverish preparation there were

still things left undone, and people were struggling at the very last minute to add to the arches of triumph which spanned the roadway at intervals or to place more flags and flowers in the windows and balconies of the houses.

The Republican troops were all wearing new green uniforms, and they had been drilled and marched until Lucilla felt their heads must be buzzing with the various orders that had been given.

All along the route that General Bolívar was to take were groups of little Indian girls dressed as multi-coloured angels holding baskets of rose-petals with which they were to shower the hero when he appeared.

There were brass bands which could hardly make themselves heard above the noise, the laughter, and the cheers of the crowd.

There were Republican flags everywhere flying from every Church, and from the houses whose balconies blazed with the colours of red, blue, and gold.

To add to the noise there were the cries of merchants selling tri-coloured cockades to put in men's hats and ribbons to hang in the pigtails of Indians, as well as patriotic songs which had been printed especially for the occasion.

On the balcony which contained the most important ladies and gentlemen of Quito, Manuela Sáenz was looking breathtakingly beautiful.

Her afternoon-gown was of white lawn trimmed with silver. It was cut so low that when she bent over the balcony Lucilla felt embarrassed.

Across her shoulder she wore a red and white moiré sash which held the gold Order of the Sun, and that was something over which Catherine could not rival her.

It would be difficult, Lucilla thought, for any two women to look more different and yet both be so beautiful.

Manuela Sáenz's dark hair and flashing eyes seemed to hold a unique loveliness until one looked at Catherine's pink, gold, and blue beauty, which made her seem like an angel from one of the gold-decorated Churches.

"How could the General fail to admire her?" Lucilla asked herself.

Even as she thought about him a rider came galloping down the street shouting:

"He is here! He is here! He is coming—the Liberator—the General! He is here!"

He tore past the houses and now everyone was pushing and fighting to be in the front row.

The Indian angels clutched their rose-petals in hot hands and the nuns who were looking after them crossed themselves and murmured: "Thanks be to God, blessed be the Virgin Mary!"

Now the whole city seemed to ring with one name: "Bolívar! Bolívar!"

It was impossible to hear the bands, the Church bells, or anything but the cry which rose in the thin air up towards the sky.

Bending foward, Lucilla could see a Squadron of Lancers advancing down the street.

They drew up in single-file on either side of the road, then in the midst of the brilliantly uniformed troops a single horseman came on alone.

It was General Bolívar riding his favourite white horse.

The animal was fidgeting and dancing imperiously, and now for the first time Lucilla could see the man who, at the age of thirty-nine, had changed, conquered, and liberated the New World.

Just for a moment she was disappointed. She had expected him to be larger, a bigger man in every way, but she could see that he was short.

Then as he bowed to the cheers and cries, as he was enveloped with the pink rose-petals, he seemed to grow in stature and she was conscious only of his deep-set black eyes, his charming, flashing smile, and white teeth beneath a small moustache.

It was obvious that he had modelled himself on his hero, Napoleon.

In contrast to his Staff Officers, who blazed with

gold braid and medals, he wore only a plain, high-collared tunic with a single medal and trousers of white doe-skin.

As he drew nearer to Lucilla he seemed to exude the power, the ambition, and the authority which had brought him to triumph and which had made him one of the most outstanding figures in the whole world.

She could sense his genius, his vision, his imagination, the brilliant strategy that had made him victorious, and somehow she felt she could understand too his amazing ability to make other men follow him and to inspire them with his own ideals.

"Bolívar!" "Bolívar!"

The people in the plaza were going mad with excitement and the little girls in their angel costumes now ran before him, scattering their petals. From all the balconies flowers cascaded down and wreaths of laurel festooned with the colours of the Gran Colombia fell at the feet of the white horse.

Just ahead of the General was the great Square where the Fathers of the City were gathered to extend to him in pompous, long-sentenced speeches the official welcome.

There were also six beautiful girls waiting to crown him with a wreath of laurel leaves sparkling with a brooch of diamonds.

The General glanced behind him and reined in his horse to allow the long line of uniformed horsemen coming behind him four-abreast to catch up with him.

Their drawn sabres were flashing in the sun and as he waited he glanced up at the Larrea balcony.

Lucilla saw both Catherine and Manuela lean forward in a sudden excitement.

Then as they both cried out his name, their red lips moving in unison, Manuela Sáenz picked up a laurel wreath and tossed it towards him.

It should have fallen at his feet but instead the wreath swung in the air and struck him on the side of the face.

The General's eyes flashed in sudden anger.

He raised his head furiously towards the culprit.

He saw her, her dark eyes wide and frightened,

a flush that stained the alabaster of her skin, her hands pressed in sudden anguish against her breast where hung the golden Emblem of the Sun.

"Forgive me!"

He could not hear the words, but he saw her lips move, then he smiled and bowed.

General Simón Bolívar, the Liberator, had met for the first time Manuela Sáenz!

Chapter Three

Not until she went up to dress for dinner did Lucilla think of her own gown.

She had been so busy these past few days with Catherine agitating over hers, and worrying about Don Carlos, that only as she finished her bath that the maids had arranged for her did she wonder what she should wear.

All the clothes she had brought from England were hanging in a large dark wood wardrobe which covered almost entirely one side of the room.

Lucilla had not nearly enough clothes to fill it, and wrapped in a bath-towel she pulled open the doors and looked at the gowns which hung there.

There were not a large number of them, most of them having been handed down at one time or another when Catherine got bored with them and altered skilfully by Lucilla to suit her slimmer figure and her own style.

This usually meant removing a large number of the trimmings with which Catherine liked to ornament all her clothes.

There was not, Lucilla thought, very much to choose from, but then she saw at the far end of the row a gown which Catherine had given her at Christmas-time, surprisingly new and unworn.

Catherine had bought it in Bond Street in the daytime and had only realised later that by candlelight the colour faded from what she had thought was a vivid blue into something softer and not so obvious.

As she looked at it Lucilla thought it was the

colour of the potato-flowers which covered so much of the ground in Ecuador, and with a smile she decided that nothing could be more appropriate.

Of soft gauze, the pale blue-grey was in fact extremely becoming to Lucilla's rather unusual looks.

It was however not surprising that few people noticed her when Catherine was in the room. It was rather like putting a very delicate, skilfully executed miniature beside a picture by Rubens and asking which would catch the eye.

Lucilla had delicate bones and only a connoisseur of beauty would have noticed the exquisite manner in which her head was set on her long neck, the straight line of her small nose, and the sensitive curve of her mouth, unlike Catherine's full, pouting, sensual lips.

But what dominated her face, which she saw herself as she looked at her reflection in the mirror, were her large grey eyes, usually worried and a little anxious.

They were worried now as she finished dressing. She was wondering if her father would think her smart enough for the occasion, knowing that in her wardrobe she had nothing better or more spectacular.

She had the feeling that he would expect her, because she was young, to wear white; moreover, white was the fashionable colour, as both Catherine and Manuela Sáenz knew, amongst the ladies who were to grace the Victory Ball.

"Nobody will notice me," Lucilla told herself, then had the sudden idea that she should visit Don Carlos.

All day long the household had been preparing for the dinner-party which Sir John Cunningham was giving before the Ball.

Everyone he had invited had been only too pleased to accept, and they were to sit down twenty-four in the long, impressive Dining-Room where the Spanish Vice-President had entertained in Royal fashion.

Lucilla's father was determined not to be outdone, and he provided the best wine, having admonished Lucilla that she must spare no expense and ingenuity in contriving dishes that everyone would appreciate.

She had done her best to carry out his orders and knew that it would be too late now to make any alterations. She was a wise enough housekeeper to know that the most important thing at this stage was to keep away from the kitchen.

She therefore had a few moments in which it would be possible to slip across the garden to the Pavilion to look at Don Carlos.

He had seemed a little better when she had visited him that morning. The lines of pain were lighter on his face and Pedro said he had not been so restless during the night.

She also thought whimsically that she would show him her gown. At least he would not be able to criticise as she had the feeling other people might do.

She arranged her hair without the elaborate curls that Catherine affected and her only jewellery was a very small string of pearls which had belonged to her mother.

She slipped out the garden-door and immediately her eyes went to the mountains which glowed golden with the rays of the setting sun.

The skies in Ecuador were a continual delight. It was still warm, the air was mellow, and there was no suggestion yet of the bitter chill that would come with darkness.

Lucilla moved through the flowers and reached the Pavilion.

Everything was looking much tidier and cleaner than it had when she had first discovered it, and she knew that Pedro found it necessary to work as near to his patient as possible.

She had a glimpse of him in the field beyond the garden and thought perhaps Francisca had asked at the last moment for more potatoes, this being something she was in the habit of doing.

Josefina was in the house, supervising the arrangements for dinner in the Dining-Room.

They had engaged extra servants for the dinner-party, and she would be, Lucilla knew, instructing them in their duties.

She opened the door of the Pavilion.

Don Carlos was lying on the floor. The sunset filled the room with a golden light and there was a large case of pink roses by him which Lucilla had picked and placed on a small table she had sent over from the house.

There was quite a lot of furniture in the Pavilion, a chest to hold the bandages and other things that were required for dressing Don Carlos's wounds, a rug to cover the floor, and a comfortable chair as well as several upright ones.

No-one would miss what was here, as Lucilla knew that neither her father nor Catherine had been interested enough to inspect every room in the house.

Almost every day she would move over something else which she thought would make the Pavilion more comfortable.

The low easy-chair was near the mattresses—there were three of them now—on which Don Carlos lay, and Lucilla sat down on the edge of it to look at him.

It seemed to her that she always saw his face even when he was not there. It still had the power to move her, as it had done the first time she had seen his portrait.

She could not explain what she felt or why he affected her differently from any other man, and yet she knew he did.

She sat looking at him as she did so often, just looking, her hands in her lap, her eyes on his face.

Suddenly, unexpectedly, as if she had called him, he turned towards her and his eyes opened.

She was so surprised, so astonished, that she could only hold her breath.

"Where—am—I?"

The words came from his lips in a low, deep tone, and yet they were clear.

With an effort Lucilla dropped to her knees.

"You are safe," she said quietly. "Quite safe."

He looked at her with the dark eyes that she remembered so well from his portrait, but she was not certain whether he saw her. She felt it must be hard for him to focus his sight after being unconscious for so long.

Then he repeated her last word: "Safe?" and it was a question.

"Quite safe," she said. "Go to sleep. You will feel better in he morning."

She put out her hand and touched his forehead where there was no bandage. It was cool, not hot with the fever as it had been for so long.

She felt that her words reassured him.

He shut his eyes, then almost like a child turned his face to cuddle it against the pillow.

Lucilla was conscious that her heart was beating frantically.

She knelt beside him for a long time, knowing that he was fast asleep and would not speak again.

But she had to go.

She went out of the Pavilion and looked for Pedro.

He was coming back from the field, carrying, as she expected, a basket filled with potatoes.

"The *Señor* has awakened, Pedro. He spoke to me."

"Then he is better, *Señorita*."

"Yes, he is better," Lucilla agreed. "Stay with him. Do not leave him if you can help it."

"I will be with him, *Señorita,* you can trust me."

"Thank you, Pedro."

She ran back to the house, afraid that her father, or worse still, Catherine, might have noticed her absence.

But they were both still in their bed-rooms and by the time they came downstairs Lucilla's breathing had become normal and her heart was not beating so violently.

It was agonising to have to sit through the dinner-party making polite conversation with the gentlemen on either side of her, knowing she would have no chance of slipping away to see Don Carlos again.

She would also have to leave with the others for

the Larrea House, where the Victory Ball was to take place.

When Lucilla had left the balcony after watching the triumphant arrival of General Bolívar, she had noticed the preparations that were being made for the evening.

She was glad that it was the Larreas and not themselves who had to cope with such large numbers.

There were carriages and sedan chairs to carry the ladies in the Cunningham party to the Larrea mansion, but the men walked accompanied by footmen carrying flaming torches to guide them through the unlighted cobblestoned streets.

Outside the Larrea mansion there was a profusion of Indian lackeys wearing a spectacular livery and knee-breeches which looked strange to English eyes, considering that the Indians were at the same time bare-footed.

The doorway of the mansion was very impressive with the family coat-of-arms carved over it in stone.

Inside, every room was flooded with light and the music of an orchestra came to the guests' ears as soon as they reached the patio.

There amongst the usual riot of flowers which scented the atmosphere there was a stone fountain of a cupid embracing a large swan. The jet of water rising from the swan's beak towards the sky was shimmering gold in the lights.

Lucilla, following closely behind her father, joined the crowd of distinguished guests climbing the wide stone staircase to the second floor.

All the young women were dressed in the latest fashion that she had seen before she left London.

Their shoulders were bared as was the vogue from Paris, their gowns moulded their high breasts, and the hems of their dresses were ornamented with lace and flowers, feathers, or silver and gold embroidery.

It was a pretty fashion despite the fact that some of the décolletages were daringly low.

Many of the Dowagers who still clung to their stiff brocades and powdered wigs looked like ghosts from another century.

The young men wore the tight trousers, strapped under polished boots, that George IV when he was Prince Regent had brought into fashion in England. With their sideburns and their hair cut in the "windswept" style, they might have stepped out of a Club in St. James's Street.

Lucilla had peeped into the Ball-Room during the afternoon when she had gone upstairs to the balcony to see the General's arrival.

It was a huge room, long and wide with tall lattice windows and a huge crystal chandelier in which hundreds of candles glowed.

The polished floor was cleared for dancing but at the end of the Ball-Room there had been erected a canopy of tri-coloured silk under which Lucilla guessed the General would stand for the presentations.

He was there, as she expected, and as she followed her father into the room she saw that unlike the simple uniform the General had worn for his arrival, he was now wearing a red military jacket, heavily braided with gold, and on his epaulettes were three golden stars.

He stood on the dais and, as she was to learn later, his polished black boots had extra high heels so that he gave an impression of height which she had felt was lacking when she saw him ride into the city.

As she waited to be presented, Lucilla thought she could understand why women found him so wildly attractive.

He was not exactly handsome, but there was something fascinating about his face and as she had thought when she saw him first, it was his eyes, deepset and penetratingly black, which were irresistible and his smile which was so captivating.

There was also something in his bearing, a courtliness, gallantry, and a hint of virility, that was inescapable.

If the gossips were to be believed, women were

as necessary to him as was food, and he could not do without them.

Everyone whispered of those he had loved and who inevitably had loved him.

There had been one who had ridden beside him, Lucilla was told, through all the terrible campaigns in the Llanos, and there were so many others—Fanny, Isabel, Anita, Bernardina—that it was difficult to believe that with so many *affaires de coeur* he had time for war.

"If I have heard so much about him," Lucilla told herself, "Catherine will have heard much more."

She knew that her sister was trembling with excitement at the thought of meeting the great Liberator.

Indeed she had talked of nothing else for the past two weeks, and now that Sir John was presenting her, she was very conscious of her looks, and sure of her attractions.

"Your Excellency! May I present my daughter Catherine."

General Bolívar took Catherine's hand as she curtseyed and looked at her with undisguised admiration.

He was always searching for beauty in women and made no attempt to hide his interest.

For a moment he looked into Catherine's eyes, until she was forced to move away as Sir John presented Lucilla.

"My younger daughter, Your Excellency!"

Lucilla felt his hand clasp hers and he smiled as he had done before, but she knew it was automatic, the courtesy and good manners of a man who had been taught in the Courts of Europe.

They moved away and others followed them.

The dancing began and immediately Catherine was besieged by a crowd of gentlemen eager to be her partner.

Some of them were the General's Staff Officers, handsome young leaders of the foreign contingent dressed in uniforms of dark green with cuffs and lapels edged in gold.

Lucilla heard that there were a number of Englishmen amongst them, and they demanded dances from Catherine as if they considered it their right.

One of them, a man called Charles Sowerby, from Buckinghamshire, asked Lucilla to dance with him.

She rose eagerly, anxious not so much to dance as to talk with him.

"It is surprising to find you here," he said.

"I might say the same," she replied.

He laughed.

"My reason is that I am addicted to war."

"I find that difficult to understand."

"There is nothing more exciting, more thrilling."

As they danced she learnt that he had fought in Russia with Napoleon's Legions at Borodino and was prepared to follow General Bolívar wherever he might lead.

"You admire him?" Lucilla asked.

"He is magnificent! The finest soldier in the world and the most delightful man to be with."

Lucilla was sad when the dance came to an end.

Charles Sowerby, who was a Colonel, introduced her to a Captain Hallowes from Kent, and he in his turn to a Daniel O'Leary from Belfast, who had been on General Bolívar's staff since he was nineteen.

It was Captain O'Leary, Lucilla learnt, who had carried the white flag to the Royalist lines during the battle at Quito and demanded their surrender.

He was only twenty-two, but she felt that age was not important when these young men had lived so fully, so violently.

They had risked their lives a thousand times, not only from the Spanish guns but also from the weather, the heights of the Andes, from malaria, dysentery, smallpox, and the privations that were inevitable for an Army on the march.

Lucilla would have liked to meet General Antonio de Sucre but he was greatly in demand among the ladies who could not catch the eye of the Liberator.

He had a delicate, sensitive face and wore huge

sideburns as if he wished to make himself look tough and aggressive.

He had left his University in Venezuela at sixteen to fight with Bolívar's guerillas and was now the greatest and most successful General of the Revolution.

He had never lost a battle, he was quiet, fastidious, and at the moment very much in love with Mariana, the lovely daughter of the Marquis de Solanda.

Lucilla could not help wondering as she moved round the Ball-Room under the candlelight what these men would say to her if they knew she was harbouring one of their enemies.

It was easy to say, as her father did, that he was not concerned in the wars or the politics of other countries but only with his business.

Yet, because so many English were serving under General Bolívar, while her sympathies were undoubtedly with the Revolutionaries, Lucilla felt guilty that she was hiding from them a man who had killed their comrades.

The Victory Ball was warming up, the wine was flowing and the voices and laughter were rising, when Lucilla saw Manuela Sáenz arrive.

She wore, as Catherine had predicted, a white organdie gown with a high waist and an even lower décolletage than she had daringly exhibited in the afternoon.

Once again there was the red and white moiré ribbon over one shoulder, engraved with its motto: *Al patriotismo de Mas Sensibles*. And under her left breast glittered the Order of the Sun.

She looked lovely, her skin translucent in the candlelight, a flush on her cheeks, her hair braided like a tiara and decorated with white flowers.

The host of the evening, *Señor* Juan de Larrea, hurried forward to greet her.

It was on his arm that she was led up to the dais, where General Bolívar still stood receiving the latecomers.

Lucilla was standing near enough to hear *Señor* Larrea say:

"Your Excellency, may I present *la Señora* Manuela Sáenz de Thorne?"

Manuela curtseyed and the General took her hand and kissed it.

Then it seemed to Lucilla as he looked down into her eyes that they were both very still.

She did not know why, but almost perceptibly she felt that something strange was happening.

It was like seeing a stone thrown into a deep pool of water and watching the ripples move out, widening, ever widening until they reached infinity.

The General said something in such a low voice she could not hear it, then Manuela moved away, but Lucilla was sure that something had happened.

Later in the evening she saw them dancing together. The General had already danced with Catherine and she had noted the excitement and the look in her sister's eyes as she flirted with him provocatively.

But he had not asked her again and now he was dancing with Manuela Sáenz and there was clearly no question of his abandoning her for another partner.

They danced together continuously. They were almost the same height and there was something not only rhythmic but almost feline in the manner in which they moved sensuously like two panthers round and round the Ball-Room floor.

Lucilla watched them.

She felt there was an affinity between them and there was a look in the General's dark eyes that told her she was not mistaken.

Sir John Cunningham did not wish to stay late. He had always hated late parties, and although it was impossible to persuade Catherine to leave, Lucilla, obedient to his suggestion, joined him as he walked downstairs.

It was not yet one o'clock and the Ball was at its height, and yet she did not mind leaving.

She had enjoyed herself and it had been delightful to meet so many Englishmen. At the same time, she was quite ready to go home.

All during the evening at the back of her mind had been the thought of Don Carlos.

She wondered if he had spoken to Pedro and she knew that actually she was longing to be beside him, to hear his voice for the first time speaking sense.

"A good party!" Sir John said as they reached home. "But all parties are inclined to go on too long."

"I agree with you, Papa."

"I doubt whether the Larreas will get much sleep tonight, or your sister for that matter," Sir John said.

Lucilla did not kiss him. He never expected it, and she knew that although he was being pleasant enough to her tonight he really disliked her and could never look at her without thinking that she should have been a boy.

"Good-night, Lucilla."

Sir John went into his bed-room and shut the door firmly behind him.

His valet, whom Lucilla had engaged for him, would be waiting for him, but there was no-one waiting for her in her bed-room.

She did not need anyone. Besides, it always embarrassed her to think that she was keeping someone waiting and therefore the sooner she went to bed the better.

Josefina had left a candle alight by her bedside and as Lucilla walked towards it to take it to the dressing-table a sudden thought came to her.

It was a revolutionary idea: Lucilla had never in her quiet, sheltered life thought of going out alone or indeed doing anything so outrageous as she was thinking of doing at this moment.

Then resolutely she opened her bed-room door very quietly and slipped down the stairs.

The court-yard and the passages were in darkness, but she found her way without difficulty to the garden-door and went through it into the garden.

There was enough light from the stars overhead

for her to see her way and the white Pavilion glowed like a pearl.

There was no light coming from the windows, because on Lucilla's orders Pedro had repaired the wooden shutters. Though it was unlikely that anyone would see it from the house, it would be a mistake to take chances and a gleaming golden light in the darkness might arouse curiosity.

Lucilla opened the door.

As she had expected, there was one candle standing on a small table by Don Carlos's bedside, and Pedro, wrapped in his *poncho,* was asleep in a corner of the room.

He slept as the Indians always did, doubled up like a pocket-knife, his *poncho* covering him like a tent, his head with his wide-brimmed hat on it tipped forward so that he looked more like a bundle than a man.

He did not move as she entered and she went quietly to the side of the bed.

She knelt down.

Don Carlos was asleep as he had been when she had left him.

She put out her hand to touch his forehead and as she did so he opened his eyes.

"You are awake?"

It was a foolish question but it came to her lips automatically.

"Who—are—you?"

His words came slowly, but then she saw a gleam of recognition as he said:

"I have—seen you—before. You came in—here and—found me—hiding."

Lucilla smiled.

"You told me you were dead, but you see, after all, you are alive!"

"Why?"

"Because we have nursed you. You were badly wounded, but now you will not die."

"You are—not Spanish?"

"No, I am English."

"English?" He looked surprised.

His eyes were on her face and he seemed to be thinking. Then he said:

"Why do you not give me over to the Patriots?"

"There has been enough killing, and I hate war!"

"I understand, and I am grateful. What is your name?"

"Lucilla . . . Lucilla Cunningham. My father has rented this house while we are here in Quito."

He seemed to lose interest, but after a moment he said:

"How soon can I get up?"

"Not yet," Lucilla said quickly. "The wound in your thigh is bad—so is the one on your forehead."

"How long have I been here?"

"Three weeks."

"It is impossible!"

"It is very possible. You were near death."

He looked away from her, frowning.

"There is nothing you can do," Lucilla said quickly, "except stay here. No-one knows you are here, and Pedro, who is the gardener, looks after you when I cannot come to you."

"Who else knows I am here?"

"No-one, except Josefina, Pedro's sister, who is a servant in the house."

This seemed to satisfy him and after a moment he said:

"I am thirsty."

Lucilla reached for the fruit juice called *Maranjilla* that Josefina had prepared for him.

It had, she thought, a delicious taste that was something between a peach and a lemon. It quenched the thirst better than anything else she had ever tried.

She put her hand behind his head and lifted it very carefully.

It gave her a strange feeling.

She had tended to him often enough while he was unconscious, but then she had felt he was only a patient, someone who was suffering and who needed her care even as a child might have done.

Now, since she had been talking to him, he had

become a man, a man whose portrait had disturbed
her strangely, a man who for some unaccountable
reason made her heart beat frantically in her breast
and her lips feel dry.

He drank and then as if the effort had been too
much for him he shut his eyes.

"Thank—you," he managed to say, and she
lowered his head onto the pillow.

He lay there without moving and after a moment or so she realised he had fallen asleep again.

"He is very weak," she told herself.

She put down the glass which contained the fruit
juice, then as she turned her head she saw that Pedro
was awake.

"If he wakes again, Pedro," she said in a whisper, "give the *Señor* some soup."

She knew that Josefina every night left hot soup
in a hay-basket so that Pedro could feed Don Carlos
if he was restless and thirsty.

Pedro nodded.

He did not move and Lucilla knew he was
keeping still so as not to disturb Don Carlos.

She rose to her feet and looked down on the
sleeping man, then turning went from the Pavilion and
back towards the house.

*   *   *

In the morning quite a number of ladies dropped
in for a cup of coffee.

They came to talk to Catherine, but as she was
not awake they sat down in the court-yard with Lucilla
and gossipped as if they could not prevent themselves from talking or telling what they had come to
tell.

It started inevitably with the General and ended
with Manuela.

They took a little time to come to the point, but
there was no mistaking that tit-bit of gossip which
they had to impart, or the fact that everyone in Quito
was quite convinced that Manuela Sáenz had spent the
night in the General's arms.

They had had supper together, then they had returned to the Ball-Room to dance with no-one but each other, until finally they had left together.

It was almost impossible for anything in Quito to happen without everyone being aware of it, and Lucilla was certain that the servants at the Presidential Palace where Simón Bolívar stayed were only too ready to talk, even without being bribed to do so.

"She was always the same, running off from the Convent when she was seventeen. Think of it—even the nuns could not contain her! And they say that after she was married, her lover joined her in Lima when her husband was away."

"What can one expect of someone who is illegitimate—whose mother was no better than she should be?" The ladies shrugged their shoulders.

They might dismiss Manuela with scathing words. At the same time, they were furious.

She had captured the hero of the moment, the man for whom all Quito was *en fête,* and they were quite convinced that she would be shameless about it and cock-a-hoop at their expense.

When Catherine eventually came downstairs she was just as incensed as were the ladies of Quito.

"It was disgusting!" she said. "That woman completely monopolised him, and I know he wanted to dance with me again. In fact he said so, but she clung to him, making an exhibition of herself, and he would be too polite to tell her to behave."

Lucilla refrained from saying that she was sure General Bolívar would do nothing he did not wish to do. She remembered that glance she had seen when Manuela was presented. Something had flashed between them that was indefinable, and yet inevitable.

It was as if, she thought, two souls who were destined for each other had met across eternity, and there was nothing that anyone could do about it.

But she was forced to listen to Catherine being spiteful with the pique of a woman who felt she had been slighted, until finally more ladies arrived, all anxious to gossip, to repeat over and over again:

"Like mother, like daughter! What else can you expect from a bastard?"

Catherine being occupied for the moment at any rate in decrying Manuela, Lucilla sought out Josefina, knowing she had been at the Pavilion.

"How is he?" she asked in a low voice.

"Better, *Señorita,* much better, but very cross when his wounds were dressed, and, like all men, raring to be back on his feet before it is possible."

"He must not move too quickly."

"He could not do so anyhow," Josefina said. "After all, he has no clothes!"

Lucilla laughed.

"So we have the whip-hand!"

"The *Señor* has a long way to go before he is well," Josefina said seriously. "He may now be able to think and speak again, but the wound in his head is deep, and it would be impossible for him to walk without his thigh bleeding."

"Then make that clear to him," Lucilla said.

She was unable to say any more because her father was calling her and it was not until *siesta*-time that she could escape to the garden.

As she neared the Pavilion she felt her heart beating excitedly and she knew that she looked forward to seeing Don Carlos more than she had ever looked forward to anything else in her whole life.

Pedro was working outside, so Don Carlos was alone in the Pavilion.

As Lucilla entered the little room, he was lying with his eyes closed, but he opened them immediately as he heard her come in.

She sat down in the low chair.

"How do you feel this morning?"

"Much better! Josefina tells me you saved my life."

"I think Josefina did that. She dressed your wounds and used the mulli resin of the Incas. We had nothing else with which to treat you."

"You might easily have handed me over to the authorities."

"As I have told you, although you may not remember it, I hate war."

"I suppose most women feel the same."

He was speaking slowly and she had the feeling that he still had to feel for his words, almost as if his head were full of clouds.

"You must not talk too much," she said gently. "Take things easily, and once you are really well again we will smuggle you out of the city and you can find your friends."

"You are very kind to me. But I have a feeling you would get into trouble if it was known what you are doing."

"No-one will know," Lucilla said confidently.

His eyes searched her face, then after a moment he asked:

"Do you know who I am?"

She nodded.

"How did you know? Were there any papers in my pockets?"

"Pedro buried your uniform," Lucilla said. "There was nothing else we could do with it."

She thought there was an expression of annoyance on his face, and she said quickly:

"I knew who you were because of the portrait in the house."

"Portrait?" he questioned.

"It hangs beside that of the President—General Aymerich."

Don Carlos smiled.

"Of course! I remember having it done. It was an infernal nuisance, but I could not very well refuse."

"It is very like you."

"I never saw it finished."

He spoke carelessly.

It was like him, Lucilla thought. At the same time, she wondered if perhaps the coldness in his eyes and his look of disdain were because he hated being painted.

"Why are you in Quito?" he enquired.

For a moment Lucilla hesitated, wondering whether to tell him the truth. Then she said:

"My father came with a ship-load of muskets and guns to sell to the Spaniards."

"And now?"

"They are still in the port of Guayaquil."

"The Spaniards would be pleased to have them."

"And so would the Patriots," Lucilla said quickly, "but it all depends upon who has the money to pay for them."

Don Carlos's lips tightened and she thought he was going to say that on no account must the Patriots have the guns. Then he said:

"Were there many weapons captured in the battle?"

"Yes."

"How many?"

Lucilla hesitated because she thought it would upset him to know the truth.

"I want to know," he said positively.

"After three Spanish companies had been destroyed, the rest broke and fled to the city."

She could not look at him as she added:

"General Aymerich surrendered. . . ."

There was silence, and then as Lucilla knew he was waiting she continued:

"About two thousand prisoners, fourteen pieces of artillery, seventeen hundred muskets, and all his ammunition and stores."

"And there were many killed?"

"The Hospitals are full."

There was silence and she wondered what he was thinking. After a moment he said surprisingly:

"Tell me about yourself."

"There is very little to tell," Lucilla answered. "My mother is dead. My father brought my sister to South America thinking she would have an amusing time in Lima because he is a friend of the Viceroy."

"Lima is in the hands of the Patriots."

"Yes . . . but we did not know that when we left England."

"So you came here."

"My sister is very beautiful. She is having a great success."

"Even though there are no dashing Spaniards to squire her?"

"There are quite a number of other men in Quito."

Lucilla wondered whether she should tell him about the Victory Ball and the Reception for General Bolívar, then she decided against it.

It might excite or, worse still, frighten him to know that he was surrounded by enemies. It was better not to mention such a thing, and she realised that Josefina had not given him the information during the morning and that she had been wise not to do so.

The most important thing after a wound in the head, Lucilla knew, was for the patient to keep as quiet as possible. Any type of shock might prove disastrous.

Although she longed to stay, she said quietly:

"I am going to leave you now. You know as well as I do that you must sleep; you should talk as little as possible."

"I feel very tired."

"You will do so for a long time, but you will get better. You are strong. Josefina says she has never known a man with such a strong body as yours."

As she spoke Lucilla blushed.

She had not meant to repeat what Josefina had said to her, but she had said it instinctively to cheer him up and comfort him.

Now she thought it had been immodest to speak to a man about his body, and the blush burnt its way up her cheeks to her grey eyes.

"Shall I tell you how grateful I am?" Don Carlos asked. "Or shall I wait until I am better?"

"Wait until you are better," Lucilla answered. "Then perhaps you will feel it is unnecessary."

"I shall never feel that. I know how much I owe you."

There was a note in his voice which made her blush again.

She rose to move towards the door. When she reached it she looked back and saw he was still watching her.

"Adiós," she said with a little smile, and left him.
Later she spoke to Josefina.

"You did not tell the *Señor* about the Victory Celebrations. I think that was wise of you. I am sure it would worry him, and he must be very quiet."

"That is what I thought, *Señorita,"* Josefina said. "He must not move, whatever happens, and if he had known that the General was here . . ."

She stopped and Lucilla said quickly:

"You are right . . . absolutely right to say nothing. I thought the same. And you have told Pedro not to speak of it?"

"Pedro never speaks of anything," Josefina replied. "If he talks, it is of potatoes."

Lucilla laughed. Then she added:

"When Don Carlos is well enough we shall have to find some clothes for him. Perhaps it would be wise for him to be dressed like Pedro and be smuggled out of the city."

Josefina did not answer, and thinking she heard someone moving, Lucilla left her quickly and went to find Catherine.

All day people had called to talk, talk, talk.

Some of the Officers with whom Catherine had danced last night came in later in the evening, and they related that the General had all day been immersed in affairs of State.

"He is creating a new Order," Charles Sowerby said as he sat in the Salon drinking Sir John's best wine.

He had come, Lucilla found, not to call on her but to see Catherine, and there was no mistaking the admiration in his eyes as he looked at her sister.

"What does that mean?" Catherine asked, not because she was interested but because she wanted to keep the attention on herself.

"It means the appointment of new Governors, new Judges, and new laws," Charles Sowerby replied. "I also heard the General say he intended to reorganise the Treasury. It is what he does in most countries he liberates, and he often chooses new names for the streets."

"There are far more important things than that,"

Daniel O'Leary said, who had also arrived, annoyed to find that Charles Sowerby had got there before him.

"What sort of things?" Lucilla enquired.

"Money—quite simply, money," Daniel O'Leary answered. "As I left the Presidential Palace, the City Fathers were arguing with the General as to why they should give up their silver plate."

"Does the General really intend to take that from them?" Lucilla asked in surprise.

"He needs money," Daniel O'Leary answered. "It is only a pity that we cannot melt down all the gold that covers the Church walls. I have never seen anything like it, except in Mexico."

"I thought General Bolívar was a very rich man," Catherine said almost petulantly.

"He was," Charles Sowerby replied, "but he has spent his own money, a huge fortune, estimated at five million, on war."

He saw that she looked surprised, and he explained:

"Soldiers have to be paid, although they often have to wait for it. Uniforms to be provided, also guns, muskets, horses, and mules; and, strange though it may seem, we all have to eat."

"I never thought of that," Catherine said simply.

"There is no reason why you should," Charles Sowerby said caressingly. "You are too beautiful to bother your little head with such mundane matters."

"Someone has to bother about them," Daniel O'Leary said almost aggressively.

"And that is what the General does," Lucilla said with a smile.

"He is fantastic," Daniel O'Leary told her. "All day, when he is not fighting, he paces up and down dictating to three secretaries at once. They are in a state of collapse and he complains to everyone that they cannot keep up with him."

"He must have extraordinary energy!"

"He has! But he likes to think that no-one can do anything except himself!"

"I expect that is true," Lucilla said.

"He does not give us a chance," Daniel O'Leary

remarked. "He has appointed General Sucre Military
Governor of the Province, but in the end he will see
to everything himself—you mark my words!"

The two men talked for some time, then more
people arrived.

Soon there was quite a party taking place and
Lucilla was busy ordering more wine to be brought
from the cellars, hurrying to the kitchen to tell Francisca to prepare more of the little delicacies and sweet-
meats that were handed round with the drinks.

Catherine was in her element, her eyes shining,
her face alight like a lovely flower.

It was not surprising that none of the men present
could take their eyes from her, and after a little
while Lucilla slipped away, knowing that no-one
would miss her.

It was hard to think of anything but the man in
the little white Pavilion who had come back to consciousness and to whom she longed to talk even
though she knew he must rest.

Chapter Four

Don Carlos was better, but he was still very weak from the wound in his thigh and his eyes hurt him when he tried to read.

Lucilla knew that he should not talk too much, and she therefore read to him during the hours she spent with him during the *siesta*.

She chose books from the Library in the house which she thought would be interesting without agitating him in any way.

She avoided all those that had to do with war.

She discovered that he, like herself, was extremely interested in art, and one day she took him a book she had brought with her from England. It described the fine pictures to be seen in Florence and the artists who had painted them.

She showed it to him and said:

"I will translate it for you, if you like."

"I can read English," he answered.

She stared at him in astonishment.

"Why did you not tell me?"

"I did not see any need for it," he answered in her own language. "You speak perfect Spanish."

"And you speak excellent English! How is that possible?"

He hesitated a moment before he said:

"I have been in England and—Scotland."

"And you liked Scotland?"

She felt that his answer was important.

"I thought it a very beautiful country."

Lucilla gave a little sigh of relief.

"It is beautiful!" she said. "I would rather be in Scotland than anywhere else in the world. The mountains, the fir forests, the burns, and the lochs somehow seem a part of me, but then I am Scottish."

Don Carlos smiled.

"The mountains are not as high as these here."

She realised he was teasing her, and she said:

"Perhaps it is a good thing. When I think of the soldiers fighting at such heights or having to cross the top of the Andes I am appalled by their sufferings."

"You are talking of the Patriots."

"I am told the Spaniards are also gathering high up on the mountains."

He did not reply, and because Lucilla did not wish him to be troubled, she quickly changed the subject.

They talked all the afternoon, but now they talked in English, which, she found to her astonishment, he could speak almost perfectly.

She thought he must have been very well educated besides having an aptitude for languages.

After this they nearly always conversed in her language, and she thought perhaps he was practising on her so that he could become even more proficient than he was already.

When she sat in the little Pavilion reading to him or, more often than not, keeping quiet while he fell asleep, she felt that she stepped into another world.

It was a world where she was alone with one man, a world that to her was like an island, quiet and sun-lit in the midst of a stormy sea.

Outside, Quito was in a turmoil.

Festivities were planned for General Bolívar every day, but all that seemed to concern the gossips was what the General did after the celebrations ended.

By that time everyone knew that when he had finished his long, exhausting consultations, the dozens of letters that he dictated every day, received the reports that came from all parts of South America, and the dinner-party or Reception of the evening was over, he sent for Manuela Sáenz.

It was only when the city was quiet and the air

was chill from the snow on the mountains that the General sent his red-haired body-guard José Palacios, who had been with him since he was a boy, to Manuela's house.

The gossips of Quito said that he wrote to her only six words:

Come to me! Come! Come now!

How they knew this Lucilla had no idea, and as a matter of fact she believed only half of what they said; but whatever the message, she was convinced Manuela Sáenz went to him.

So many people had seen her with their own eyes, moving through the streets to the Presidential Palace, covered by a large dark cloak, guided by Palacios's hurricane lamp and protected by his two huge dogs.

Because Lucilla was a young girl, what happened in the Palace was inferred by her rather than put into words by others.

Yet when she was alone she would think about those two people making love in the great vast rooms where the President had ruled in State, and she found it difficult to put them out of her thoughts as the night passed.

It seemed to her, although she knew she was very ignorant on the matter, that when two people loved each other, the pomp and circumstance and the rank and trappings of glory were of no importance.

It was not the great General, the Liberator who had been crowned with laurel leaves and diamonds, who held Manuela Sáenz in his arms, but a man—a man whose heart had reached out to her heart and who needed her as she needed him.

And when Manuela was close beside him, loving him and being loved, Lucilla felt that all the unhappiness and the tumultuous scandals of her girlhood were forgotten.

The Convent from which she had been expelled, the lover with whom she had run away, the dull, unimaginative man to whom she was married—none of them were of any consequence, all that mattered was love and the fire that blazed between them like a burning furnace.

Because she was rather shocked at herself for thinking such things, Lucilla felt she could never speak of the General or of Manuela to Don Carlos.

He would not understand, she thought, and she went again to look at his portrait on the wall, wondering why, even now that she knew him, she felt there was some inner reserve, some withdrawal into himself.

Then unexpectedly, although there were many more entertainments planned for him, General Bolívar left Quito.

Everyone expected Manuela to go with him, but instead immediately after he had gone she started to make herself necessary to him by organising the provision of all that he needed.

The gossips were astonished, having forgotten, if they had ever known, that in Lima besides her secret carrying of seditious proclamations she had also organised the other women who wished to help the Patriots.

With them she had collected money with which to build ships. She had even managed to canvas from house to house to obtain *pesos* to buy uniforms.

In Quito she set herself the same task, only now it was more urgent, more important, and closer to her heart.

She descended like a whirl-wind on the ladies of Quito. Every house was turned into a factory where both the noble ladies and the Indian servants slaved at making uniforms for the new Army.

Manuela started a collection for money, jewels, gold and silver plate, and every other type of valuable with which she intended to finance General Bolívar's next campaign.

The ladies complained of her autocratic methods not only in making them work but in extorting from them treasures which they did not wish to hand over.

"She actually blackmails people into producing jewels and silver from their safes," they whispered.

They hated Manuela's slave Jonatás, a light-skinned Negress who they said learnt from other servants secrets which people wanted to keep hidden.

Everyone knew that General Bolívar had gone to Guayaquil to meet General San Martín and it might easily end in another battle.

It was said by those who trusted Bolívar that he would be too clever for San Martín. In fact, Lucilla learnt that he had hurried south towards Guayaquil with all possible speed, changing horses at every opportunity, because he knew that the advantage of the meeting would fall to him if he arrived at Guayaquil first.

Lucilla remembered what the journey had been like when she had driven from Guayaquil to Quito and she wondered what the Liberator felt as he rode along the chain of breathtaking, shining snow-capped peaks with Chimborazo rising to twenty-one thousand feet and showing its gleaming cone far above the high rising clouds.

Then when she thought of General Bolívar she had another thought to trouble her.

Her father had not finally clinched the deal over his ship-load of fire-arms.

Lucilla knew without being told the reason why the cargo had not by this time exchanged hands.

It was simply because General Bolívar had not the money to pay and Sir John would not give him credit.

They had talked; in fact, Sir John had gone to the Presidential Palace not once but half-a-dozen times in the week before General Bolívar had left.

There was no doubt that the Patriots were desperate for weapons. Even those which had been surrendered to them at Quito were not enough, and besides, the General had other Armies to think about, all of which were writing incessantly for money, for provisions, and for arms.

Because Lucilla was sensitive to other people's

feelings and because she listened to everything that
was being said round her, she knew that General Bolívar stood at the cross-roads in his great and adventurous life.

It really depended on his first taking Guayaquil
and then consolidating the whole of Peru.

Everyhing in fact had worked out successfully
up to this moment when by his brilliant strategy the
Spaniards had been driven north as he liberated one
after another of the South American countries.

For thirteen years General Bolívar had fought
through the mountains, the plains, the jungles, the
deserts, and out of it all had come at last the thing
he had dreamed of—a great Republic with already the
provinces of Venezuela, Panama, and now Ecuador
united into the Federation of what he called Gran
Colombia.

It was incredible that one man, even one with
such amazing energy and vision, should have achieved
so much, but there still remained a question mark over
Guayaquil.

Before he left, General Bolívar had said quite
openly:

"Whoever controls Guayaquil controls the whole
of Ecuador. The difficulty is that Peru claims it belongs
to them."

Lucilla longed to discuss such matters with Don
Carlos, but she knew it would be unwise.

For one thing, she was afraid he might hate her
for the fact that her allegiance was now quite certainly with the Patriots.

She might be English, and she might, as her father said, be officially neutral, but her whole heart
and soul longed for the Liberators to win and for the
Spanish to be completely and utterly beaten.

Yet how, she asked herself, could she reconcile
such thinking with what she felt for Don Carlos?

She was not in fact quite certain what she did
feel, she only knew she wanted to be with him.

She wanted desperately for him to be well; at
the same time, she could not face the thought that

once he was well he would leave and she would never see him again.

She forced herself not to show any sign of the conflict within her mind when she sat by his bedside and read to him.

Sometimes they would discuss something she had said, but at other times he would just lie still, looking at her with his dark eyes until either she finished what she was reading or he fell asleep.

Now, a week after the General had left, he was so much better that he insisted on sitting up, and Lucilla thought that when no-one was with him he tried to walk.

"How bad is the wound in his thigh?" she asked Josefina.

"It is nearly healed, *Señorita,*" Josefina replied. "The mulli has worked its usual miracle as it has healed from the bottom. If we had had a doctor he would have put stitches, many stitches, into the wound, but the good God gave us mulli and the magic in it has healed great warriors since the beginning of time."

Lucilla knew she was thinking of the Incas and she wondered whether perhaps they had in fact known more than modern science teaches.

After all, it was the Incas who had discovered quinine, which cured malaria, and potatoes, and many fruits like avocados and strawberries.

All the precious cereals on which the Indians lived had originally been grown by the Incas on the terraces which they built up the sides of the mountains.

She talked about them to Don Carlos and she found that he knew so much about the ancient civilisation which had been destroyed by the Spanish that she was fascinated by what he had to tell her.

"How could they have done anything so cruel, so wicked, as to destroy such wonderful people?" she had asked.

Then she remembered that in saying "they" she really meant "you—the Spanish."

"It was cruel," he agreed quietly, "cruel and quite unnecessary. But you must remember that the first Spaniards to come to this country were rough and un-educated men who had been taught only to take life, never to preserve it."

Lucilla felt that nothing could justify the way they had behaved, but she did not say so aloud.

Instead she picked up the books she had brought with her and placed them on a small bookcase which was another new addition to the little Pavilion.

"How do you occupy your day when you are not with me?" Don Carlos asked.

"I have my father's house to run," Lucilla replied, "and my sister, who is very beautiful, always wants new gowns and is very rough with the ones she has already."

"You mean the young men with whom she dances are rough," Don Carlos said with a smile.

That was the truth, Lucilla thought. Catherine's laces were always torn, her gauze skirts frayed at the bottom, the delicate embroidery in need of repair, mainly because of the new waltz which had just been introduced from Europe.

"I would like you to see my sister," she said to Don Carlos. "She is very lovely—as lovely in her way as *Señora* Manuela Sáenz."

Don Carlos started.

"Manuela Sáenz is here?" he asked.

Lucilla realised she had made a slip.

"Yes . . . she came here from . . . Lima."

"I am surprised to hear that," he said, and she thought he was frowning.

Hurriedly Lucilla placed the books on the shelf and rose to her feet."

"I must go."

"Good-bye, Lucilla, and thank you."

She felt there was something cold in the way he spoke, as if his thoughts were elsewhere, and she had a feeling that she had perturbed him by speaking of Manuela Sáenz.

Why? What did she mean to him? Did he suspect

that she was one of many things she had kept from him? Lucilla wondered.

The following day she went to the Pavilion, two books in her hands which she was eager to discuss with Don Carlos, to find him on his feet.

She gave a gasp as she went into the Pavilion, then saw that he was wearing the uniform of the Patriot Army, the tight, dark green trousers of an Officer, the tunic gold-trimmed, and though he had not put them on, standing on the floor were a pair of black patent-leather Wellington boots.

"You are up!" she gasped.

He looked rather pale and thin, but his smile flashed out as he replied:

"As you see."

"But . . . why? And why are you wearing . . . those clothes?"

"Josefina thought they were the most sensible gear in which I should ride out of town."

"Yes . . . yes . . . of course, but why did she not tell me?"

Lucilla was angry—angry that she had not been told by Don Carlos or Josefina what they were planning.

"I am surprised that you should condescend to wear the uniform of your enemies," she said aloud.

"I can hardly wear my own, as I hear it is buried several feet under ground," Don Carlos replied.

"No . . . of course not," Lucilla agreed.

She was silent for a moment, then she forced herself to say:

"It is, of course, a wise precaution if you wish to make your escape. There are soldiers everywhere and you would not get far unless you were disguised."

"Then surely nothing could be more effective than this?" Don Carlos asked.

He spoke mockingly, then quite suddenly he sat down on one of the chairs.

There was a blue look round his mouth, and without saying anything Lucilla rose and went to a table on which stood a bottle of wine.

She poured out a glass and handed it to him.

He took it from her and drank it.

"You are doing too much too quickly," she said as the blue look vanished and the colour came back into his face.

"I know," he answered, "but there are things that have to be done."

"If your wounds start bleeding again, you may be laid up for weeks. Please be sensible."

"I have been sensible for a long time."

"I know," Lucilla agreed. "I know it has been hard, but there was nothing else you could do."

"I could have died, except for you," he answered.

There was something in his voice that made her feel embarrassed.

"Will you have another glass of wine?" she asked quickly.

"No, thank you," he replied. "I think if you will call Pedro I will go back to bed. I had been walking up and down before you came, strengthening my muscles, and I do feel very tired."

Lucila gave one quick look at him and hurried to get Pedro.

When Don Carlos was in bed she went back to the Pavilion.

He lay with closed eyes and she was not certain whether he was asleep or whether he did not wish to talk.

The uniform he had been wearing lay over a chair and she wondered from where Josefina could have obtained it, then thought she had doubtless stolen it or bribed another servant to do so from the store of uniforms that Manuela Sáenz was building up in the Presidential Palace.

Every day the little social factories in the grand houses of Quito sent finished garments across the Square, vying with one another as to who could contribute the most to the Army of Liberation.

*   *   *

A few days later Lucilla went to the Pavilion to find Don Carlos up and dressed.

There was also a soldier's pack on the floor which she had not seen before, and she had the feeling as she entered that he had been packing it with various things including sandwiches. One packet was still lying on the table.

She stood looking at him, then she said, hardly above a whisper:

"You are . . . leaving?"

He nodded his head.

"Pedro is arranging for a horse to be waiting for me in half-an-hour's time. It is best to leave now so that I can be some way from Quito before it grows dark."

"Where are you going? How are you sure that your own people will not shoot you while you are dressed like that?"

"That is a chance I have to take," he answered, "but at least I will not be shot before I leave the city."

He put the last packet of sandwiches into his pack and set it down on a chair.

He had his Wellington boots on and he looked, Lucilla thought, very tall and distinguished.

The green uniform suited him better than the blue and gold in which she had first seen him, and quite as much as the formal white tunic in which he had been painted.

He was still very thin, but the dark lines under his eyes which came from pain had vanished, and she thought in some ways he looked younger.

He opened a drawer of the chest and took out some money which Lucilla knew Josefina had taken from the pockets of his Spanish uniform before it was buried.

A little diffidently, but knowing she must say it, Lucilla asked:

"Have you enough money? I could let you have some."

He smiled and it took the hardness from his face.

"I have taken so much from you already, Lucilla," he said. "And I still have enough pride not to ask a woman for money."

"I am offering it."

"I know that. But the answer is no."

"If you are deliberately depriving yourself through pride, it is very stupid of you," she said sharply. "This is a very dangerous moment in your life, as you well know, and the only thing that matters is that you should get to safety."

"To fight again—is that what you are suggesting?"

She drew in her breath.

"I am not suggesting anything that you should do once you leave here. All I want is to be sure that you reach wherever you are going."

"That is generous of you, considering that your instincts lead you to support the Patriots."

"How . . . do you . . . know . . . that?" she asked a little incoherently.

"Why did you not tell me that General Bolívar was here in Quito?"

Lucilla looked away from him.

"I suppose Josefina has told you that now. We decided it might upset you. You were desperately ill. To be agitated or worried might have been fatal!"

"What you are really saying is that I might have been frightened."

"No . . . of course not. At that same time, I knew it would upset you to know that the General had taken over Quito."

He smiled at her as if she were a child.

"You are a very unusual person, Lucilla," he said, "and I thank you for thinking of my feelings, just as I thank you for making me well, for not letting me die or handing me over to the military."

"It is because I have gone to all that trouble, for which I do not want to be thanked, that I am begging you now to be very, very careful," Lucilla said. "Remember, you must not ride far today because of the wound in your leg. You must not become overtired or worried, or you will have one of your headaches again."

"I will try to remember everything you have said to me," Don Carlos replied, "in fact I am quite certain I shall remember."

"Then . . . please try to be . . . sensible," Lucilla begged.

As she spoke she heard a long, low whistle.

It came from the direction of the potato field, and she knew it must be a signal from Pedro to let Don Carlos know that he had a horse waiting for him.

She stood looking at the man towering above her and he seemed to fill the whole of the small room in the Pavilion.

It was difficult to realise that he was going away after they had been together for so long. She had been alone with him in a manner in which she had never before been alone with a man, but now he was moving out of her life and it was most unlikely that she would ever see him again.

She wanted to grasp the whole impact of it, but instead she could only think of how handsome he was, how authoritative, how he had a presence which made her feel he would stand out in a room of other men.

"I must go."

He said the words quietly, and yet there was a purpose behind them which she did not miss.

"You will take care of . . . yourself . . . and remember what I have . . . said?"

"I have promised you, and I will do that."

"Then God go with you. I shall be . . . praying for you."

"I would like to think that you were doing that."

"I shall be praying all the time."

Her lips were speaking words that somehow had no meaning. All she could think of was that he was leaving, and every nerve in her body cried out against it.

She wanted him to stay, she wanted things to go on as they had been. She did not wish to lose him.

He put out his hand and, hardly aware of what she did, she put her own into it. Then as she looked up at him, her eyes wide and worried seeming to fill her whole face, she thought there was something different in his expression.

"*Adiós!*"

His voice was very low. Then as if he could not prevent himself he drew her nearer to him and as his arms went round her his lips came down on hers.

She was not surprised; she was not even startled. She just felt it was inevitable, something that had to happen.

As she felt the hard pressure of his lips she felt something warm and wonderful rise up inside her and move through her from her quickly beating heart into her throat.

It was so perfect, so miraculous, that it was part of the beauty of the mountains, the sky, the flowers, of everything she had felt since she had come to Quito.

She knew now it was what she had longed for and what she had felt belonged to her since she had known Don Carlos.

How long he kissed her she had no idea, she only felt as if the small Pavilion was suddenly invaded by a brilliant light more golden and more dazzling than the sun, and that her body melted into his and she was a part of him as he was a part of her.

Then as the whole world swam dizzily round her, he set her free.

"Good-bye Lucilla," he said in English, and his voice was hoarse.

He went from the Pavilion before she could move.

She stood where he had left her, then slowly, very slowly, her hands went up to cover her eyes as if she could no longer bear the golden radiance which had enveloped them both and which had now gone.

"I love him!" she told herself wonderingly.

She heard her voice whispering the words and they seemed to echo and re-echo and come back to her from the small walls which had for so long enclosed a dream.

*   *   *

Afterwards Lucilla could never remember how she got through the days which followed.

It seemed to her as if she moved through a haze

and that a fog like the clouds that covered the mountains enveloped her so that she could neither see nor hear clearly what was happening round her.

All she was conscious of was the feeling that Don Carlos's mouth was still on hers, that his lips held her captive, and his arms clasped her to his heart.

She was conscious of him in the daytime as she moved and spoke like an automaton. At night she thought that she lay in his arms, and she recaptured the sensations, the rapture, and the wonder he had brought her with his kiss.

"I love him!" she told herself not once but a thousand times, and knew that she would never love anyone else.

She was sure that she was the type of woman who loved once and only once in her life, and since the wonder of it had come and gone she would live only with a memory.

She did not rebel against the thought. She was humble enough to know that while he filled her whole life to the exclusion of all else, she in fact could mean nothing to him.

For one thing, she was an enemy; for another, she was a foreigner; and she was sure that if there were women in his life they would be like Catherine or Manuela Sáenz, brilliant, beautiful women—birds of Paradise who would be his equal in every way.

And yet he had kissed her. It might have been just in gratitude, she was not doubting that that was the reason for it. At the same time, it had transformed her from an insignificant girl who had no opinion of herself into a woman who glowed with the wonder, the beauty, and the ecstasy of love.

She felt as if she had changed overnight into someone very different from who she had been before.

Because no-one paid any attention to her in the house except for the servants—for her father never looked at her if he could help it, and Catherine was entirely absorbed with her own interests—no-one noticed any difference, but Lucilla knew it was there.

She had only to look at her eyes in the mirror to

see that they shone with a strange radiance, and her face seemed to have changed too.

It seemed fuller and more alive, and she felt that the sunshine of the mountains and the flowers spoke of her love just as they had seemed part of the kiss that he had given her, which had been as beautiful as the mountains and flowers were.

"I love you, I love you!" she said to the portrait which hung in the room inside the entrance hall.

She went to look at it a dozen times a day, and, though she felt it did not portray the real Don Carlos whom she now knew, it brought him back to her so vividly that it gave her the feeling that he was still near her and that she was a part of him.

'He will never think of me again once he is free,' she thought, but she knew that for the rest of her life she would think of him and love him with her whole being.

Because people seemed to talk to her through a fog, she was barely attentive when as dinner ended her father said:

"What time do the servants go to bed?"

"To bed, Papa?"

"That is what I asked you!"

"I am not certain," Lucilla answered. "When they have finished their duties they go into their own part of the house. I presume they either go to bed or go out into the town."

She did not understand why he was interested and she looked at him in perplexity.

"Why do you wish to know, Papa?"

"I have someone calling on me tonight," he answered, "at about eleven o'clock. I would rather the servants did not open the door."

Lucilla looked at him in surprise and after a moment she said:

"What are you suggesting?"

"I am suggesting it would be best if you let my visitor in," Sir John said slowly. "If you stayed in the room near the door, you would hear a knock, would you not?"

"Yes . . . of course, Papa."

"Then do that. Do not ask the man's name nor have any conversation with him. Just bring him to my Study."

"Y-yes . . . Papa."

Lucilla was astonished but she did not like to ask questions.

Sir John turned towards the door, then he said:

"See that there is wine in the Study and make sure that we are not disturbed."

"Yes, of course, Papa."

She gave the orders for the wine to Josefina.

"Is the *Señor* expecting visitors?" she asked.

"No . . . I do not think so," Lucilla answered, "but if he is, he will bring them back to the house himself, and there is no need for anyone to wait up."

"Very good, *Señorita,* and there is nothing you require?"

"No, thank you, Josefina."

They were alone in the Salon and Lucilla asked in a low voice:

"You have not heard . . . anything?"

There was no need to explain, and Josefina shook her head.

"No, *Señorita*. We have heard nothing. Would you wish Pedro to bring the things back from the Pavilion into the house?"

Lucilla considered for a moment, then she said:

"No, leave them for the moment Josefina. They might be needed again—who knows?"

Josefina said nothing, but went from the Salon.

It was ridiculous, Lucilla told herself, and yet somehow she hoped, she even prayed, that one day Don Carlos might come back.

She did not ask how it was possible or why he would wish to do so. She just knew that as her prayers went out to protect him from danger, so without putting it into words her whole being prayed that she might one day see him again.

Because the room in which his picture hung was near to the entrance hall, when it was after half-

past-ten Lucilla moved from the Salon to sit in a
leather-covered writing-chair at the Vice-President's
desk.

She placed a candelabrum with three candles in
front of her, and by their light she could see Don
Carlos's portrait very clearly on the opposite wall.

It seemed almost as if he were walking out of the
frame towards her: she shut her eyes and imagined
his arms were round her and his lips were on hers;
and she felt again the wild ecstasy of love.

Carried away by her thoughts, she felt herself
jump when there was a knock on the door.

It was not imperative, just a rather quiet knock
given, she felt, by someone who did not wish to draw
attention to himself, and yet expected to be let in.

She rose quickly, and carrying the candelabrum
because the servants had extinguished the lights in
the entrance hall, she went to the great door.

There were bolts to be drawn back, keys to be
turned, and when finally it was opened, she saw a
man wearing a dark cloak almost like a monk's
robe.

In fact for a moment she thought he was a monk
or a Priest.

"Sir John Cunningham?"

"He is expecting you," Lucilla replied.

The man moved quickly through the door, so
quickly that Lucilla had the idea he was afraid he
might be seen.

She pushed home one of the bolts, then setting
the candelabrum down on the table escorted him into
the court-yard.

Here the lights were still lit and she led him along
the flagged patio to her father's Study.

She opened the door and the man went in.

She heard her father say:

"Don Gómez, I am delighted to welcome you."

Outside the door, Lucilla stood very still.

So the stranger was a Spaniard!

She might have expected it, and now she was
quite certain that the reason for so much secrecy was
that the Spaniard had come to discuss with her father

the sale of the weapons that were still in the ship at Guayaquil.

At the thought of it she suddenly felt frantic.

She wanted those arms to go to the Patriots. She wanted it desperately.

She knew from what the young men like Charles Sowerby had said how greatly they were needed and how far superior in every way the Spaniards were in military equipment.

'Papa cannot do this,' Lucilla thought.

She reached out and very softly pushed open the small peep-hole with which most Spanish doors were furnished.

It was a precaution against enemies and unwelcome visitors, to be found on the outer doors of every house in Quito.

It was also in this particular house a feature of the doors which opened onto the court-yard, and now as Lucilla eased with her fingers the small square piece of wood, she found she could hear what was being said inside the Study.

"You have not yet sold your fire-arms to the Rebels, Sir John?" Don Gómez was saying.

He spoke good English but with a distinct accent.

"No, they have not been able to meet my price," Sir John replied.

"Then let me tell you that we are prepared to pay anything you wish to ask."

"My cargo, as you know, is at Guayaquil and General Bolívar is there."

"We may have to ask you to take it to another port."

"That would not be difficult," Sir John said, "but it would in consequence cost more."

"That is understood."

"You are very confident that you require these weapons," Sir John said slowly. "I understand the Patriots, or as you call them the Rebels, are now in complete control of Ecuador besides a number of other countries."

There was a moment's pause before Don Gómez said:

"It is a position, Sir John, that is soon to be reversed."

"Really? Do you expect me to believe that?"

"You may believe it for the very simple reason that General Bolívar's Army will soon be completely annihilated."

There was a pause and Lucilla felt she could almost see the supercilious smile on her father's face.

He had been impressed by the General, she knew, and she thought the Spaniards might find it hard to make him believe that he could be so easily defeated.

"I will convince you by telling you one thing," Don Gómez said as if he also sensed that Sir John was sceptical.

"What is that?"

"We have discovered that the reason for our recent defeat at the hands of the Rebels was the presence of a spy in our ranks who informed General Sucre of our exact military position before the battle of Quito. He was also incidentally instrumental in bringing about our reverses in other countries."

"How is that possible?"

"Because he was in a position of trust with the Spanish Commanders and in their confidence," Don Gómez answered. "He was a friend of President General Aymerich, and a confidant of the Viceroy of Peru and of the Viceroy of Granada."

"And you say he was a spy?"

"His real allegiance was to Bolívar!" Don Gómez said, and Lucilla heard the fury in his voice.

"And having discovered this, you really believe that you can turn such defeats into victory?" Sir John asked.

"I will tell you what we intend," Don Gómez said. "We intend to leave him in ignorance that his perfidy has been discovered. We will feed him with information as we have done in the past."

He paused to say impressively:

"He will sit in on the conferences of the Generals and the Viceroys and he will lead Bolívar into a trap—a trap set by us with the skill and brilliance that has been part of the glory of Spain in the past."

There was a note almost of exaltation in his voice and Lucilla felt that her father must be impressed.

"When will all this take place?" Sir John asked.

"At any moment," Don Gómez replied. "We have just found it a little hard recently to locate this man. His name is Don Carlos de Olañeta. You will find, Sir John, that he was one of the most important men in this city before his treachery turned the battle of Quito into a disaster as far as we were concerned."

"I seem to have heard the name," Sir John murmured.

"Everyone knows Don Carlos," the Spaniard said. "Everyone until now has respected him and even admired him. But all the time, like Judas Iscariot, he was betraying us—betraying us to Bolívar and his ramshackle army of beggars and slaves!"

Don Gómez spoke passionately and after a moment Sir John said:

"I am certainly interested, *Señor,* in your suggestion that I should sell my cargo to you. At the same time I can see, for the moment, some practical difficulties."

"Which will be eliminated after the battle of which I am speaking has taken place."

"Then it would obviously be wiser to wait. After all, what is a week, two weeks? I am quite comfortable here and the guns will suffer no damage as long as they are in the hold of my ship at Guayaquil."

"We appreciate that, Sir John," Don Gómez said, "but may I have your word that once the battle takes place, once Spain is victorious as she undoubtedly will be, the arms will be delivered immediately on the payment of whatever price you wish to ask?"

"That is a promise I can give you easily," Sir John said. "And I presume I shall be informed?"

"Of that you may be sure," Don Gómez agreed.

"Then let us drink to a very amicable arrangement," Sir John said.

Lucilla felt that he raised the glass that he held in his hand and now she crept away from the door in her soft, heel-less slippers.

She felt cold with shock and fear. At the same

time, she was frantically wondering what she should do.

Don Carlos was a Patriot! Don Carlos was in danger!

That was all she could think of and it seemed to go round and round in her head.

She knew now that she should have told him that General Bolívar was in the town. But how was she to know, how could she have guessed for one moment that, wearing a Spanish uniform, and being of such importance that his portrait hung next to the President's, he was really supporting the Liberator?

Yet her heart was singing because he was on the same side as she was, the side of justice, the side of the people against the Imperialists.

As she reached her own room she found to her surprise that there were tears on her cheeks and knew they were tears of thankfulness.

The last shadow over her love had gone, the shadow of knowing that he was an enemy of all she believed in, all she admired. He was not only a comrade but incredibly, marvellously brave.

She could almost see as if he were telling her how hard his rôle had been to hold the complete confidence of the Spanish, and yet to help General Bolívar, fighting desperately for the freedom of South America—for his vision of the Gran Colombia.

"He is wonderful! Wonderful!" Lucilla sobbed.

Then suddenly her tears ceased.

It was not enough to know that Don Carlos was all she wanted him to be—she had to save him.

The Spaniards intended to use him, intended to destroy through him the Army of the Liberators. But as they did so they would also destroy the man who had betrayed them.

"I must save him!" Lucilla said aloud.

She had left her door open and now downstairs she heard footsteps in the court-yard and knew that her father was showing Don Gómez out.

It was not yet half-past-eleven and she knew it would be impossible to go to bed and wait for another day to dawn before she did anything to save the man she loved.

'I must do something quickly ... now,' she thought.

For a moment she felt helpless and her brain did not work.

Then she thought of the one person whom she must tell of what was happening, the one person who would be in a position to save Don Carlos.

Manuela Sáenz!

She went to the door of the room and heard her father coming upstairs to his own bed-room.

Sir John always disliked late nights and even half-after-eleven was quite a late hour for him.

Lucilla waited until she heard his door shut, then going to the wardrobe she took down her dark travelling-cloak which was lined with fur.

It had once belonged to Catherine and was therefore much more luxurious than anything she could have afforded to buy for herself.

She pulled it over her shoulders, then moved quietly down the stairs and through the court-yard towards the servants' quarters.

The kitchens were ablaze with light and she could hear the twang of a musical instrument and thought that the staff would be sitting round the big kitchen-table, drinking the cheap Ecuador wine which they enjoyed.

She hesitated for a moment, then she called out: "Josefina!"

There was a sudden silence amongst the chattering voices. Then there was the sound of a chair scraping against the flagged floor and a moment later Josefina came out of the kitchen.

"Did you call, *Señorita?*"

"Yes, Josefina, I wish to speak to you."

Josefina moved forward so that she was out of ear-shot of the other servants. Then she said as if she sensed something was wrong:

"What is it, *Señorita?*"

"I will tell you later, Josefina," Lucilla said, "but

now I have to go immediately to find *Señora* Manuela Sáenz. Where will she be?"

"I think, *Señorita,* she will be in her own house. I will send Gustavo and Tomás with you. They know the way and they will carry torches."

"Thank you, Josefina, and no-one must know I have left the house—you understand?"

"Of course, *Señorita.*"

She felt without words that Josefina knew this was somehow connected with Don Carlos, but there was no time to tell her what she had learnt.

Instead she moved quietly across the court-yard to wait in the dark entrance hall, hoping that Catherine would not come home before she left.

It was only a few minutes, although it seemed longer, before Tomás and Gustavo appeared, both carrying flaming torches that were used in the streets of Quito at night.

Josefina came with them.

"They know where to take you, *Señorita,*" she said in a whisper. "I will wait up and let you in when you return."

"Thank you, Josefina."

She went out through the heavy door and heard Josefina push the bolt into place when they had gone.

When Catherine returned home, she always rang a bell that echoed through the house, waking the servants and everyone else.

But usually it was dawn before she came back from a Ball or Reception and by that time the younger servants were up, sweeping the court-yard and pulling back the curtains in the Salons.

The cobbled street was deserted, and walking in the centre of it with one of the men on each side of her Lucilla set out to walk briskly down the hill into the main part of the city.

There were few people about and the only sound was the cry of the night watchmen—*"Ave Maria,* a June night. All is well."

It seemed a longer walk than it really was, because Lucilla was so frantic to reach Manuela Sáenz and to set in motion the rescue of Don Carlos from what she knew would be certain death.

She had saved him once from dying and now she must save him again. But this time it was even more frightening because he was involved with the whole Army of Liberation and with the whole structure of the Gran Colombia.

She reached Manuela Sáenz's house and to Lucilla's relief every window was bright with lights.

She might have guessed, she thought, that Manuela Sáenz would not go to bed early. At the same time, she hoped there would not be a large party there so that her arrival would be gossipped about all over Quito.

It would mean she must have some plausible explanation for calling so late.

A servant let her in and Lucilla said:

"I wish to speak to *Señora* Manuela Sáenz—and alone. Would you be kind enough to tell her it is of the utmost urgency."

The servant showed no surprise, as if he was in the regular habit of relaying such urgent messages. He merely showed Lucilla into a small room which was well lit although it was obviously not in use, and hurried away.

He was gone for what seemed to Lucilla to be so long that she was afraid that perhaps Manuela Sáenz would refuse to see her, and she might have to do something more to gain her attention.

Then suddenly the door was flung open and she stood there, looking extremely beautiful in a gown of crimson silk which made her dark, flashing beauty even more spectacular than it had usually been.

She walked into the room to stare at Lucilla for a moment as if she did not recognise her. Then there was a smile on her face and her hand went out.

"Miss Cunningham—I could not think who wished to see me at this hour."

"You may think it . . . strange," Lucilla replied, "but I have something of great importance to tell you . . . something which I think you should know about at once!"

She thought her hostess looked unimpressed and she added quickly:

"It concerns General Bolívar!"

A different expression came over Manuela Sáenz's face, and opening a door in the room that Lucilla had not noticed before, she led her into a comfortable Salon where there was a fire burning in the grate.

The candles were lit and for a moment Lucilla stared about her, thinking she must be dreaming.

The whole place was like an Aladdin's cave. On every table, on every chair, and even on the floor, there were treasures of every sort and description.

There were silver and gold plate, goblets, candlesticks, ink-pots, every type of vase, and great piles of silver dishes bearing the crests of the most illustrious families in Quito.

There were also velvet and leather boxes which Lucilla knew contained jewels, harnesses for horses that had been made of gold, snuff-boxes set with diamonds, and a whole multitude of other things all of which she knew were very valuable.

She realised this was the collection which she had heard Manuela was making from the families and Churches of Quito in support of General Bolívar's Army.

Going nearer to the fire and tipping some boxes first from one chair, then another, Manuela Sáenz made a gesture with her hand.

"Sit down, Miss Cunningham, and tell me why you have come."

She seated herself opposite Lucilla and in the firelight her gown glowed like a ruby and her dark eyes were mysterious and sensual.

Lucilla drew a deep breath.

"I have come," she said, "to tell you what I overheard in my father's house tonight and which concerns Don Carlos de Olañeta."

The surprise in Manuela Sáenz's expression was obvious.

"Don Carlos?" she exclaimed. "But how could you know anything about him?"

"I have learnt from what I overheard that he

supports General Bolívar even though everyone thought he was a Spaniard working with his own countrymen."

"Tell me what was said," Manuela Sáenz suggested.

Almost word for word Lucilla recounted to her Don Gómez's conversation with her father.

She finished speaking, then she added:

"I knew there was only one person I could tell . . . and that was you! Perhaps General Bolívar will know where Don Carlos has gone and can warn him."

"What do you mean—where Don Carlos has gone?" Manuela Sáenz asked.

Lucilla blushed.

She had forgotten that she had not explained her own connection with Don Carlos.

"He was wounded," she said, "desperately and dangerously wounded. I found him in the Pavilion at the bottom of our garden."

"So that is where he has been," Manuela Sáenz said. "The General was wondering what could have become of him."

"I presume he had somehow been involved in the battle of Quito," Lucilla murmured.

"That is likely, or else he was trying to get away after General Aymerich surrendered. He would not have wished to be taken prisoner."

"No . . . of course not," Lucilla agreed.

"So—you kept him hidden all this time."

"Up until seven days ago."

"How did he go?"

"Our gardener found him a horse and he was wearing the green uniform of the Patriots."

"In which case," Manuela said, "he will join General Bolívar. In fact, I am certain he will be at Guayaquil."

"If you know where he is, will you send him a message immediately?"

There was a silence, as if Manuela Sáenz was thinking.

What Lucilla did not know was that she was in fact rather amused.

Carlos Olañeta had always been spoken of as a

cold man, unlike his compatriots, not particularly concerned with women. There had been no scandal attached to him.

His name had never been connected with the high-ranking ladies who fawned on him in Quito or Lima. In fact, he had shown no particular preference for any of them, Manuela Sáenz thought, not even herself.

She remembered an incident when Carlos Olañeta had made it quite clear that he was not interested in her.

It had rankled because he was perhaps the only man who did not respond to any encouragement she might offer him.

And she had not forgotten.

It was the sort of thing Manuela Sáenz was not likely to forget, and yet, she thought, Don Carlos, the fastidious, the imperious, had been at the mercy of this pale, not particularly attractive girl.

She did not admire Lucilla, who was so different from her spectacular, beautiful sister.

It suddenly struck her as rather funny that of all the women who might have soothed his fevered brow, it was this little nonentity who had done so, rather than a legion of lovely, sophisticated, bewitching creatures who would have been only too proud and glad to be in her position.

Lucilla was watching Manuela Sáenz anxiously.

She had the feeling that something was holding her back. She could not understand what it was, but she was sure it was stopping her from going immediately to the rescue of Don Carlos.

Suppose they were too late? Suppose already the battle was in progress and Don Carlos had led General Bolívar into the trap which had been set for him by the Spaniards?

She felt as if she must scream out at the very urgency of it. Then Manuela Sáenz spoke.

"We must certainly warn Don Carlos," she said, "and we must also warn General Bolívar."

"You will send messengers immediately to Guayaquil?"

Lucilla, although she was afraid she might be

thought impertinent, could not keep the urgency out of her voice.

"Yes, I will send messengers," Manuela agreed, "but you, Miss Cunningham, must go with them."

"What do you mean? I do not . . . understand," Lucilla said.

"Who else except yourself can tell them what is planned? You are the only person who has heard what was said and what is to be done. If Carlos Olañeta is to be saved, then you, Miss Cunningham, must save him."

"I . . . but how can I? How is it . . . possible?" Lucilla cried.

Manuela Sáenz rose to her feet.

"You must leave at dawn," she said. "It will take you nearly eight days to reach Guayaquil. There are places where you can stay on the way, and although they may not be very comfortable, you will be safe."

She paused, then she said:

"I will send a Squadron with you."

Lucilla sat staring at her open-mouthed.

"So that you will look less conspicuous," Manuela Sáenz went on. "I will lend you one of my riding-habits cut in military fashion. We are almost the same size, although you are thinner. You had better come upstairs with me while I fetch it."

"B-but I . . . cannot," Lucilla stammered. "I cannot . . . do this."

"You have to!" Manela Sáenz said positively. "You have, Miss Cunningham, not only to save one man but a whole Army. Could anything be more important?"

The question was asked.

"N-no . . . no . . . of course not!"

"Then leave me to make the arrangements; and, as I have already said, you must leave at dawn."

Chapter Five

Riding over the excruciatingly bad roads as the sun rose to turn the land in front of them to gold, Lucilla thought she must be dreaming.

She could hardly believe this was really happening and that it was not some figment of her imagination or a wishful desire to see Don Carlos again.

Manuela Sáenz seemed to sweep her along like a tidal wave: she had no time to think or to feel but just did what she was told, as if she was propelled into action by a force greater than herself.

While she was still gasping and almost incoherent at the idea of going herself to find Don Carlos to tell him what she had overheard Don Gómez saying to her father, Manuela Sáenz had taken her upstairs to her bed-room.

"I presume," she said with a note like contempt in her voice, "that you would not ride astride?"

"No, of course not!" Lucilla said quickly.

She was aware that Manuela Sáenz had shocked and horrified the Dowagers of Quito by coming into the town astride her horse, wearing a pseudo-military uniform which made her look like the soldiers who escorted her.

It gave them something at which they could throw up their hands in horror, and it was only the beginning of their condemnation of her, which increased on every occasion they saw her, culminating in her love-affair with Simón Bolívar.

Now as she moved across the bed-room in her crimson gown it was difficult for Lucilla to think of her as anything but an excessively feminine and extremely attractive woman.

Then as she pulled open the wardrobe to stare at the rows of multi-coloured garments inside it, she turned aside for a moment to pick up a small cigar from a box on a side-table and light it.

Puffing fragrant smoke into the air, she turned again to the wardrobe and drew from it a bottle-green riding-habit with, Lucilla saw, thankfully, a full skirt, but with the jacket cut in a military manner and decorated on the shoulders with gold-tasselled epaulettes.

"This should fit you," Manuela Sáenz said, throwing it down on a chair, and from the shelf above the gowns she took down a gold-trimmed Officer's képi.

"Will they not think it strange for me to be dressed like that?" Lucilla asked in a low voice.

"It will draw less attention than if you wear the type of pale-coloured habit I suspect you have brought with you from England," Manuela Sáenz answered.

She did not wait for Lucilla to reply but asked sharply:

"Can you shoot a pistol?"

Lucilla's eyes opened wider than they were already, but she answered:

"My father taught both Catherine and me to fire one of his before we left England."

"Then I will lend you mine," Manuela Sáenz said. "They are downstairs."

Carrying the habit and the képi in her hand, Lucilla had followed Manuela Sáenz down the stairs to be given in the entrance hall the pistols of which she had spoken.

She stared at them apprehensively. They were two enormous brass Turkish pistols, engraved on the brass mountings with their owner's name.

"Let us hope you do not have to use them," Manuela Sáenz said as if she sensed Lucilla's hesitation. Then she added:

"Hurry back and be ready to leave at the first break of day."

"Clothes ... I shall need ... clothes," Lucilla stammered.

"Of course," Manuela replied. "One horse will carry panniers and there should be room in them for a gown or two, but you had best travel light."

"Yes ... of course," Lucilla agreed.

The two men who had escorted her through the city were waiting outside the front door, and lowering her voice so that they could not hear what she said, Lucilla asked:

"What am I to say to my father?"

Manuela Sáenz considered a moment, then she replied:

"Tell him you are staying with friends. If he objects, there is nothing he can do about it. Though you cannot tell him so, it is his fault you are involved."

"If I had not overheard what was said," Lucilla said, "General Bolívar's Army might have been led to destruction."

"I am aware of that," Manuela Sáenz said sharply, "in which case your personal problems, Miss Cunningham, pale into insignificance. Just do as I have told you and you will be able to save Don Carlos and with him the Patriots."

"Yes ... yes, of course," Lucilla answered.

She had gone back to her house, her escorts carrying the pistols while she hid Manuela Sáenz's strange riding-clothes under her long cloak.

Josefina was waiting to let her in and she hurried upstairs to her bed-room, telling the maid to follow her.

"What is happening? What is all this about, Señorita?" Josefina asked. "Why have you brought back those clothes and the pistols belonging to Señora Sáenz?"

Her shrewd eyes had missed nothing and Lucilla saw the worried expression on her face as she turned to say:

"I have something to tell you, Josefina. The Señor was not, as we thought, a Spanish Officer."

Josefina gave a little smile.

"Yes, I know, *Señorita*. He supports our beloved General and our own people."

"You knew?" Lucilla exclaimed.

"*Sí, Señorita.*"

"Then why did you not tell me?"

Josefina shrugged her shoulders.

"Servants know many things they dare not say, *Señorita.*"

"And you have known this for a long time?"

"*Sí, Señorita,* but had we spoken of it, not only the *Señor* but we too would have lost our lives."

Lucilla drew in a deep breath.

"I am so glad . . . so very, very glad, Josefina, that his . . . sympathies are not, as I thought, with the Spaniards. But he is in danger . . . grave danger!"

Josefina did not speak but Lucilla saw the horror in her eyes.

"The Spaniards have discovered that he has been deceiving them," Lucilla said in a low voice, "but do not intend that he should know it. They plan to trap him with false information which might prove disastrous for General Bolívar. I have told *Señora* Sáenz and she says I must go at once and warn Don Carlos and the General."

"She wants you yourself, *Señorita,* to go!" Josefina exclaimed incredulously.

Lucilla nodded.

"She thinks it is important and I must do as she says."

Lucilla thought Josefina was going to protest. Then almost as if she bit back the words Josefina said in a strange voice:

"When do you leave, *Señorita?*"

"As soon as it is light," Lucilla answered, "and I have very little time, Josefina. Will you pack for me what I require? I have to ride to Guayaquil."

"It is a long way, *Señorita.*"

"I know," Lucilla answered, "but it is important I should reach the *Señor* with all possible speed."

"Yes, of course, *Señorita.*"

Josefina hurried about the bed-room, pulling

open the drawers and taking down gowns from the
wardrobe.

"I cannot take much," Lucilla said nervously. "It
will all have to go in two panniers on a horse's back."

"There will be a number of things you will need,"
Josefina said firmly.

She began to pack what seemed to Lucilla an
inordinate amount of clothes, but later, to her relief,
they all fitted into the panniers.

She was afraid that Catherine might see her de-
part and protest or probably arouse her father to speak
to her; but fortunately at about two o'clock Lucilla
heard the bell clanging in the kitchen-quarters.

"That will be *Señorita* Catherine," she said to
Josefina.

"Blow out your candles, *Señorita,* until she has
gone to her room," Josefina ordered. "If she thinks you
are awake she might come and talk to you."

Lucilla thought it unlikely. At the same time, it
would be a mistake to take any chances, so as Josefina
ran down the stairs to answer the front-door bell, she
blew out her candles.

A little while later she heard Catherine coming
up the stairs and moving along the open patio of the
court-yard to her own room.

She was yawning and she made no reply to Josefina's respectful: *"Buenos noches, Señorita."*

Lucilla heard Catherine's bed-room door close, and
as she lit her candles again Josefina came into the room.

They made no reference to Catherine, and Josefina said:

"Lie down on your bed for a little while, *Señorita.*
You have a long way to go and it will be very tiring.
Try to sleep if you can. I will wake you the moment
the soldiers are here."

"They will not ring the bell?" Lucilla asked
quickly, fearing that it might arouse her father or
Catherine.

"Gustavo is already waiting at the door and will
let me know the moment anyone is in sight, and he
will warn the soldiers to be as quiet as possible."

"Thank you, Josefina, you think of everything," Lucilla said.

She was already dressed in the full bottle-green skirt belonging to Manuela Sáenz's riding-habit.

She had on her feet her own patent-leather riding-boots and one of her own white muslin riding-blouses with its soft white muslin cravat twisted high round her neck.

The military jacket was waiting for her on a chair and she had arranged her hair tidily and closely to her head to wear under the Officer's képi.

She lay back carefully against the pillows and Josefina covered her with a light blanket.

"Sleep, *Señorita*," she said. "You have a long journey in front of you."

It was impossible for Lucilla to relax completely, because her heart was beating frantically in her breast.

She kept thinking apprehensively of what lay ahead, questioning whether she was right to do what Manuela Sáenz had virtually commanded. Yet she knew it was right, as she had said the only thing that really mattered was to save Don Carlos and the Patriot Army.

How could she have known or even guessed that he was not what he had seemed to be?

Her heart was singing because now she knew she loved him even more than she had before, because he was so brave, because he had undertaken one of the most dangerous and nerve-racking missions that any-one could possibly imagine.

She was thinking of him when Josefina came back into the room and drew the blanket gently from her.

"The soldiers are in sight up the street, *Señorita*," she said.

Lucilla gave a muffled exclamation and sprang out of bed.

"There is no need for hurry, *Señorita*," Josefina said quietly. "They will wait. Gustavo will tell them you are coming and there are your clothes to be placed in the panniers. Tomás is seeing to that."

Early in the evening while Josefina was sorting

out the things she would take with her, Lucilla had
written a note to her father.

In it she had said very little. She had merely explained that she had been invited to a Victory Ball at
Guayaquil with some friends who were leaving early
in the morning and had offered to take her with them.

She hoped he would understand why she did not
wish to miss such an historic and exciting occasion,
and as soon as it was over she hoped to return with
her friends and would therefore be quite safe and well
looked after while she was away from home.

She signed it, forcing herself not to think how
angry he would be when he read it.

Never in her whole quiet life had she ever taken
an independent action or in fact done anything of
which he would disapprove. For one thing, she had
always been too frightened of him.

In fact she had never been tempted to rebel
against him simply because there was nothing that she
felt strongly enough about to take the initiative.

She knew that her father and Catherine expected
her to be a willing slave, ready to do anything that
was asked of her and having as far as they were concerned few thoughts or feelings of her own.

But this was different. This was something about
which she felt passionately. This was something she
knew she intended to do although the whole world
might try to prevent her.

"Give my father this note when he wakes, Josefina. I hope he will not be angry with you for helping
me leave," she said.

"I know nothing—I can say nothing!" Josefina
replied.

Lucilla had given her a little smile.

"I know already how secretive you can be," she
answered, "because you never told me that you knew
Don Carlos was a Patriot."

"He is a very brave man, *Señorita*," Josefina said
in a low voice, "a brave man and a good man. We
have always admired him."

On an impulse Lucilla bent forward and kissed the
maid on the cheek.

"Thank you for looking after him . . . and me,"
she whispered. "I shall be back as soon as I can. I
hope Papa will not be too angry with me."

Her voice shook for a moment as if she was
afraid, then resolutely she put Manuela Sáenz's képi
on her head and thought how becoming it was.

Josefina handed her her riding-gloves and a thin,
narrow whip that she had brought with her from England.

They tiptoed down the stairs, Lucilla moving
slowly because the gilt rowels on her spurs tinkled as
she walked.

Everything seemed unnaturally loud in the quiet,
sleeping house and there was only the soft fall of the
water from the fountain to break the silence.

They reached the front door and as Gustavo
opened it Lucilla saw waiting outside there was a
Squadron of soldiers, as Manuela Sáenz had promised
her.

They were dressed in the new uniforms that had
been made for the arrival of the Liberator, but they
were still bare-footed with the exception of a Sergeant
who was in charge of them.

He saluted and Lucilla gave him a little bow and
a smile, but did not speak.

"Good-bye, Josefina," she said in a low voice,
and allowed Tomás to help her onto her horse.

It was a spirited bay, prancing and fidgeting a
little as if he was in need of exercise. Then as soon as
Lucilla had her knee over the pummel and Tomás
had arranged the fullness of her skirt, the soldiers
moved off.

Lucilla was a good rider, but having been unable
to ride for two months she knew that it was going to
require all her strength and resolution to reach Guayaquil.

However, for the moment it was sheer joy to be
in the saddle again and to feel the cold air gradually
disappearing as the sun rose in the sky and the
clouds which covered the mountains began to disperse.

It was so beautiful and the loveliness of it seemed
to be echoed by the excitement within her.

She could not believe that she was doing anything reprehensible or indeed outrageous, because she was possessed of a strange enchantment.

It was as if she left behind her old self, as a snake sheds its skin, in the darkness of her bed-chamber in Quito, and was now a new and unknown Lucilla journeying towards her heart's desire.

That was what Don Carlos was, she told herself, and although she was well aware she could never mean anything to him, it was enough to know that she was saving him, helping him as she had helped him before, saving his life for the second time.

Her only terror was that she might not be in time or that things had not gone right at Guayaquil.

It was too soon to know what had happened at the meeting between General Bolívar and General San Martín.

When she wrote to her father that she was going to a Victory Ball, she thought that she was merely anticipating the truth.

But the fear was still there that Guayaquil would wish to stay under the protection of Peru and not accept the Federation of Gran Colombia as Bolívar hoped they would do.

It was all rather alarming. At the same time, something within Lucilla that she had never known about herself before leapt like a flame at the thought of being part of the action that was taking place, part of the vision of General Bolívar himself as he fought and strove for the liberation of his country.

"How could I ever have been content with the dull, uneventful life I have lived so far?" Lucilla asked herself.

She knew that in a way she had been asleep, moving through the days with only a small part of herself alert and alive.

Now she was awake, awake not only to the dangers and difficulties which surrounded her but to the possibilities within herself.

They rode swiftly over rough roads, through narrow mountain-passes, and into an almost uninhabited land where the only people to be seen were an occasional few Indians guarding a flock of sheep or half-a-dozen llamas.

Lucilla loved the strange animals with their long necks and their gentle, rather foolish faces.

She knew that as beasts of burden they were the only carriers that could survive the great heights of the Andes and the thin air which had not enough oxygen in it for man or beast.

The shepherds paid little attention to the soldiers and about midday they stopped for a meal at a small *hacienda* where there was a slightly better-educated Indian who welcomed them politely but not effusively.

Lucilla felt he had seen too many changes and too many different types of visitors in the last few months.

He was suspicious of them both—Spaniards and Patriots—and all he wanted was to farm his land and preserve his herds in peace.

Nevertheless, he allowed them to use his stove to cook their food and Lucilla knew that the Sergeant had brought enough with them for two days.

After that they must rely on what they could purchase.

Lucilla had fortunately not only a certain amount of her own money which she had not had time to spend since arriving in Quito, but also the housekeeping money.

She had not paid the servants that week, or the tradesmen's bills. It amounted to quite a considerable sum and she told Josefina to ask her father for more.

It would annoy him but at the same time he would certainly pay up, and no-one would suffer through her appropriating the money which was not really intended for her in the first place.

She told the Sergeant that she would pay for everything they ate, but she had the suspicion that even so the soldiers would commandeer what they needed as a matter of right.

They rode steadily on, and Lucilla was extremely tired and feeling very stiff by the time they reached the *hacienda* where they were to stay for the night.

She realised it had all been mapped out for her

by Manuela Sáenz and could not help admiring her organisation, which was efficient down to the last detail.

Again it was only an Indian farm at which they stayed. The bed was hard and very uncomfortable, but Lucilla was too tired to mind.

The most inconvenient aspect was that there was no water with which to wash: water in this part of the world was so scarce and precious that the Indians did not waste it on washing. This was why, Lucilla realised, they and their children invariably looked so dirty.

The soldiers provided blankets for her bed and to cover her she had her fur-lined cloak which Josefina had arranged to be fixed at the back of the Sergeant's saddle.

With the things that she had brought in the panniers of the horse, she managed to make herself comfortable, and the moment her head touched the pillow she fell asleep, not even having time to think of Don Carlos.

When she awoke she realised that she was stiffer than she had ever been before in her life and longed for a hot bath to ease away some of the ache in her limbs—but that of course was impossible.

Soon she was back in the saddle and they were riding at the same speed as they had ridden the day before.

The first two days were very painful and at times an agony, but before long Lucilla realised that her body had adjusted itself to the unusual exercise and she managed to get out of bed lithely.

They stayed in many strange places, only one being an Inn, which Lucilla had visited with her father on their way from Guayaquil to Quito.

She realised they were keeping off the usual beaten track and she thought it was a wise precaution.

The soldiers frequently looked apprehensively over their shoulders and glanced towards the rocks and nearby hills as if they were afraid of a hidden enemy.

On and on they went until Lucilla felt they would be travelling forever and Guayaquil would never come in sight.

Then at last, when she least expected it, she saw the sea and a number of ships and knew they were not far from the port.

Now, Lucilla thought, they would soon know the worst: whether General Bolívar had been successful, or whether when they reached the town they would find no welcome for them.

They reached the outskirts and she saw again the houses on stilts of split bamboo and the dirty, dusty streets which had shocked her on her arrival in South America.

Before they had gone far, the Sergeant drew the Squadron to a standstill and stopped to ask for information.

Now Lucilla could see triumphal arches of palm leaves over the roads and the colours of the Gran Colombia festooning the balconies. She was sure without being told that General Bolívar was the victor.

The Sergeant came to her side.

"It is good news, *Señorita*," he said with a smile on his olive-skinned face.

"Good news?" Lucilla questioned, although she already knew the answer.

"Guayaquil is ours and General San Martín has returned to Peru."

"That is indeed good news, Sergeant! But is General Bolívar here?"

"He has moved to a *hacienda* outside the town, *Señorita*. We will go there."

"Yes, Sergeant, let us go there immediately!"

They turned their horses and rode towards the mountains in the distance.

It did not take long to get away from Guayaquil into the countryside.

Now everything was fresh, clean, and bright again, and Lucilla could understand the General not wishing to stay in the squalid, dirty port.

They saw the *hacienda* before they reached it and as they drew near there were soldiers—soldiers everywhere, drilling on a flat piece of land, polishing and repairing their weapons, giving the impression that they were preparing themselves for further action.

'We are in time!' Lucilla thought, and felt her heart beating with relief.

Every day she had become more and more anxious that she might be too late.

She had a feeling that the moment his meeting with San Martín was over, General Bolívar would return to his main activity of fighting the Spanish.

She was sure that they also were preparing and that their well-equipped Army would not be far away, hidden in the mountains and having, even without the information from their spies, a very accurate idea of what was happening along the coast below them.

Some of the soldiers smiled and waved at comrades as they passed, then they had entered the wall which enclosed the *hacienda* and were moving among shrubs until they came to a big court-yard round which the farm was built.

It was in the pattern of all Spanish farms, but it was well painted and luxurious. Lucilla suspected it had been occupied by a rich and perhaps noble Spaniard until very recently.

A soldier helped her to dismount and she moved through an archway and walked towards the steps where she thought the main part of the house must be.

There were sentries outside an inner door and as they looked at her curiously an Officer appeared and Lucilla recognised him. It was Colonel Charles Sowerby.

He stared at her in astonishment before he said, almost as if he could hardly believe his own eyes:

"Miss Cunningham—is it really you?"

Lucilla held out her hand.

"I have come from Quito."

"Why? I mean—we were not expecting you."

His astonished eyes took in the way she was dressed, and because she could understand his surprise, Lucilla gave a little laugh.

"It is unexpected," she said. "But I have come to ask if Don Carlos de Olañeta is with you."

Colonel Sowerby was still.

"Don Carlos de Olañeta?" he repeated.

"I have to see him immediately. It is of the utmost importance!"

"I do not know what to say," Charles Sowerby murmured after a moment's pause.

"Please take me to him . . . if he is here," Lucilla said. "If he is not . . . we have to find him."

Colonel Sowerby looked at her uncertainly, then he said:

"Will you come with me?"

He took her inside the house and almost for the first time Lucilla realised how hot it had been for the last few hours and how cool the house was in contrast.

The windows of the room were shielded by the patio outside, and the dimness after the brilliance of the sunshine outside increased her sense of relief at having arrived after travelling for so long.

"Will you wait here, Miss Cunningham?" Colonel Sowerby was saying in a grave tone.

He shut her into a comfortable Sitting-Room where the furniture was of a high quality.

There were rugs on the floor and it was, in fact, Lucilla was certain, the home of someone of distinction and taste.

She was suddenly conscious of herself and the way she looked.

Because she felt nervous and shy, she smoothed back the tendrils of her hair and hoped she did not look too hot or that her skin was sun-burnt.

She was in fact not as pale as she usually was, and there was a faint golden glow over her face which was very becoming.

She pulled off her riding-gloves and laid them down with her whip on a side-table. She hoped that Don Carlos would not think she looked as strange as Colonel Sowerby obviously had done.

Even as she thought of him the door opened and he came in.

She turned her head swiftly, then as her eyes met his she found it impossible to move and hard to breathe.

"Lucilla! You really are here!" Don Carlos said. "I thought Charles Sowerby must be joking when he said you wanted to see me."

"I . . . I have come to . . . warn you."

He walked forward towards her.

"To warn me?"

She raised her eyes to his and thought he looked more handsome, more impressive, than she remembered.

"You are all right? It has not been . . . too much for you?" she asked impulsively.

He smiled.

"As you see, I have reached here—but how did you know where to find me?"

"*Señora* Manuela Sáenz was sure you would be here."

"Manuela! So she is at the bottom of this!"

"I went to her when I learnt that . . . you were not . . . who you . . . appeared to be."

"How did you learn that?"

Lucilla hesitated a moment, then he said:

"Forgive me, you must be tired. Sit down. I will bring you something to eat and drink. That is of more importance than anything else."

"No . . . it does not matter," Lucilla said. "I wanted to tell you . . . but I was so . . . afraid . . . so desperately afraid that I would not be . . . in time."

His eyes were on her face but he did not speak, and after a moment she said:

"A man came to see my father . . . a Spaniard . . . and I heard him say that they had discovered your . . . sympathies were with the Patriots and General Bolívar."

"Who was the man?"

"His name was Don Gómez."

"I know him—go on!"

"He said they would set a . . . trap for you . . . give you false information for you to pass on. Then they would . . . defeat the General and his Army."

"He told your father all this?"

"He wanted to buy the weapons that my father has in the ship in the harbour here."

"I understand," Don Carlos said. "You overheard what was being said and went at once to Manuela Sáenz."

"She was the only person who I thought would be able to help," Lucilla said simply.

"And she sent you here to me?"

"She said I must tell ... you what I had ... overheard ... that you might not ... believe it unless I came ... myself."

She saw an expression in Don Carlos's face which she did not understand, and she asked quickly:

"Was it ... wrong?"

He did not answer and after a moment she continued:

"Perhaps it was ... stupid of me. I could have ... written it all down and the soldiers could have brought it to you in a letter. I did not think of ... that."

There was something almost piteous in the way she spoke, and Don Carlos said quickly:

"No, no! You were right to come and it was very brave of you. I do not know of any other woman who would have been courageous enough to come from Quito as you have done."

"There was no ... time to think of doing ... anything different," Lucilla said in a low voice.

Then suddenly there was an expression in his eyes which told her that he thought it strange that Manuela Sáenz had sent her to him.

She looked away from him, suddenly shy, the colour rising in her cheeks.

"Sit down," Don Carlos said insistently.

Lucilla obeyed him automatically and he went to the door. She heard him giving orders to a servant outside.

He came back and sat down on the sofa beside her.

"I am very grateful, Lucilla," he said quietly. "Were you very surprised when you learnt that I was not what I pretended to be?"

"I was happy ... glad. It had always seemed to

me to be wrong that you could support the Spaniards in their cruelty and oppression of the people."

"I would have liked to tell you," he said. "I thought of it when you sat reading to me, or we talked those long afternoons when you never mentioned what was happening in the city outside."

"I thought it would upset you to know that General Bolívar had won the battle and was celebrating the victory," Lucilla said quietly.

As if she must explain herself further, she said almost passionately:

"You were so ill ... so desperately ill. For several days I thought you would die."

"It is thanks to you that I am alive."

"And to Josefina, who told me just before I left that she knew you supported the Patriots."

"She knew that? How could she know?"

"She said servants know more than people think. But an unwary word—and both you and she would have been executed!"

There was a little throb in Lucilla's voice that was unmistakable.

"It is all over now," Don Carlos said, "and let me tell you again how brave you were to have come here and saved me for the second time."

It was what Lucilla herself had hoped she was doing, but she did not have to reply, for at that moment a servant came into the room.

There was the cold, delicious *marajilla* to drink which she had given him when he was ill, and because she had been very hot and very thirsty long before she arrived at the *hacienda,* she thought that she had never tasted anything so delicious.

"Will you excuse me," Don Carlos asked, "if I go and tell the General the information you have brought me?"

"Yes, of course," Lucilla said, "and the Sergeant has letters for him from *Señora* Sáenz."

"He will be pleased to have those," Don Carlos said.

He went from the room and almost as soon as he left Charles Sowerby came back.

"You have certainly given us a surprise, Miss Cunningham," he said. "You must not think it rude if I say you are the last person I should have expected to be so brave or so adventurous."

Lucilla knew she should take it as a compliment; but at the same time, she was aware that he had supposed that because she was so insignificant and so unobtrusive as a rule, she would never have taken such an initiative.

She did not answer and Charles Sowerby went on:

"It is a shame that we shall not be able to use Carlos in the same way in the future. He has been magnificent! Simply magnificent in the way he has helped us to turn what might have been a dozen defeats into resounding victories."

"I wonder how they discovered the truth," Lucilla said.

Charles Sowerby made a gesture with his hand.

"Heaven knows! Anyone might have given him away a hundred times before now. He had to trust servants, runners, other spies, while the Spaniards are always prepared to pay for information, far more than we can afford to do."

"They are trying to buy the weapons my father has in the ship in the harbour," Lucilla said in a low voice.

"I might have guessed that," Charles Sowerby replied. "The General told me your father would not deliver the goods unless he had the money actually in his hand, and God knows we cannot find that much at the moment."

"What happened at the meeting with General San Martín?" Lucilla asked.

She wanted to change the subject, thinking it embarrassing that her father should be so rigidly businesslike when Englishmen like Charles Sowerby were risking their lives to help what they believed was a just and glorious cause.

"General Bolívar, needless to say, was superbly confident!" Charles Sowerby answered. "He arrived here some days before the schooner *Macedonia* came from Peru carrying San Martín. He rode into the city

and led us in a victory march through the streets. He
used what he himself called 'charm and surprise' to
win over the leaders of Guayaquil."

He laughed before he went on:

"They capitulated without a fight, and when San
Martín arrived, expecting conversations, negotiations,
and concessions on both sides, General Bolívar greeted
him with the words:

" 'Welcome, My General, to the soil of Gran
Colombia!' "

Lucilla gave a little cry of sheer delight.

"He must have been astonished!"

"He was; at the same time, he has aged and has
been taking opium for some time, because of pains in
his stomach. He is also racked with rheumatism."

"Poor man!" Lucilla said.

"I agree," Charles Sowerby said. "But it makes
him slow and cautious. He does not want to fight. He
wants the peace and quiet which he thought he would
gain by taking Peru."

"What happened after that?"

"San Martín pulled himself together, determined
to be heard. Then General Bolívar gave him a letter
that had just been received from Lima. There had
been a Palace Revolution!"

Lucilla listened wide-eyed as Charles Sowerby
continued:

"The day after San Martín left for Guayaquil, the
other members of the Government had thrown those
they disliked out of the city and promulgated a new
provisional Constitution."

Charles Sowerby smiled rather cynically as he
went on:

"It was the typical reverse that those engaged in
politics have to accept. San Martín attended the Victory
Ball, but left abruptly, and as General Bolívar followed him he said: 'I have finished my public life.' I
shall go to France and live out my days in retirement.' "

"Oh, poor man! It is almost too cruel to bear!"
Lucilla exclaimed.

"I agree," Charles Sowerby said, "but I cannot be

sorry that Guayaquil, which is so important, is now part of Gran Colombia."

"No, of course not!"

The door opened and Don Carlos came into the room, and with him was General Bolívar.

Lucilla and Charles Sowerby rose to their feet.

The General crossed the room, holding out both his hands.

"Miss Cunningham," he said. "Olañeta has told me how amazingly courageous you have been. How can I thank you?"

He took both her hands and raised them one after the other to his lips.

"I do not think I ever appreciated the English until this moment," he said quietly. "Although I have always known that their women were beautiful, I did not expect them to show such fortitude or indeed such amazing courage."

Lucilla blushed.

"Thank you," she said, "but I want to congratulate Your Excellency on the acquisition of Guayaquil. Colonel Sowerby has been telling me all about it."

"As I would like to tell you myself," General Bolívar said, "may I ask you to dine with me *Señorita?*"

Lucilla was about to reply when in a cold voice Don Carlos interposed:

"Miss Cunningham came to see me, My General!"

The General's eyes went to him and there was both a glint and a twinkle in them.

Just for a moment he did not speak, then with a twist of his lips he said:

"Is it possible that your invulnerability is at an end, Carlos?"

Don Carlos did not answer, and the General said:

"Of course, the invitation to dine is extended to you as well."

"Thank you, Sir. I have much pleasure in accepting it," Don Carlos replied.

The eyes of the two men met. Lucilla did not

quite understand what was happening, but she felt
that without words Don Carlos conveyed something to
the General that he accepted, though there seemed to
be some tension in the atmosphere.

Then turning to her the General said:

"You will wish to rest, and I dine at eight. I shall
see you then, Miss Cunningham, to proffer my thanks
more fully than I am able to do at the moment."

He kissed both her hands again, then went from
the room and Charles Sowerby followed him.

A little nervously Lucilla looked at Don Carlos.
There was a frown between his eyes and after a moment he said:

"As you well know, you should not be staying
here unchaperoned. But there is nothing I can do
about it except to safeguard you in every way I can."

"Safeguard me? But why . . . and from whom?"
Lucilla asked in surprise.

Then quite suddenly she understood and the
blood flooded into her cheeks.

The General had asked her to dine with him.

She had heard of his reputation with women when
she was in Quito, but since she knew of his attachment
to Manuela Sáenz, it had not struck her for a moment
that there was any likelihood of there being any other
woman in his life, least of all herself.

But now, almost like a bomb-shell, she understood what Don Carlos had meant when he said she
had come here to see him, and why the General had
seemed amused.

Feeling agitated and embarrassed, she turned her
back on Don Carlos and walked towards the window.

She stared out into the sun-lit court-yard and after a moment she said:

"I should not . . . have come . . . I realise that
now. I think perhaps *Señora* Sáenz intended to em-
barrass you . . . by my presence here . . . but why?"

"You are imagining things," Don Carlos said
slowly. "As I have already told you, Lucilla, I am extremely grateful and so is the General. It is just that a
beautiful woman is always a liability in time of war."

A beautiful woman!

Lucilla felt that she could not have heard the words aright. Then she turned and saw an expression in his eyes which made her heart beat violently—so violently that it seemed to jump from her breast towards him.

"You are very beautiful, Lucilla!" Don Carlos said almost as if he spoke to himself. "And therefore the sooner you go back to Quito, the better!"

Chapter Six

There was a discreet knock on the door and Lucilla awoke with a start.

"It is half-after-seven, *Señorita*," a voice said, and she remembered where she was.

She had been dreaming that she was still riding—riding, riding, until she thought she would never reach her destination.

But now she knew she was here! She had told Don Carlos what she had discovered. She was actually under the same roof with him and he had called her beautiful.

At the thought of the way he had spoken, she got out of bed hastily to put on the gown that had been carried in one of the panniers on the horse's back, and make herself look as attractive as possible.

She had bathed before she rested, washing away the dirt of the *haciendas* in which she had slept and the clouds of dust that had risen from the roads to linger on the thin air long after they had passed.

When she looked at herself in the small mirror in her bed-room she was far from satisfied with what she saw.

How could anyone think she was beautiful, she wondered, in comparison with Catherine or indeed with Manuela Sáenz?

She was surprised to find that Josefina had packed one of her best gowns. Though it was not particularly elaborate nor in the least spectacular, it became her and seemed part of the soft, gentle image that had been the Lucilla she knew before she started adventuring.

She could only hope that Don Carlos would not be disappointed, but when she went into the Sitting-Room where he was awaiting her, she could not tell from the expression on his face what he was thinking.

He asked her conventionally if she was still tired and hoped the rest had done her good.

Before they had time to exchange more than commonplaces, the door opened and General Bolívar came in, and with him was a very beautiful girl.

Lucilla was surprised, as she had not expected to find another woman in the *hacienda* after what Don Carlos had said to her.

The General introduced them.

"Miss Lucilla Cunningham—*Señorita* Joaquina Garaycoa."

Lucilla curtseyed and Joaquina did the same.

"The *Señorita* and her sisters, who live in Guayaquil, have been most kind and hospitable to me since I arrived," the General explained. "I call them my angels, and no-one could deserve the description more."

He spoke with an almost passionate intensity and when they went in to dinner in his private Dining-Room Lucilla watched him wide-eyed while he showered Joaquina Garaycoa with compliments, flattering her and making what seemed to Lucilla to be almost passionate love while she looked at him adoringly with her dark-fringed eyes.

The General had so much to say that Lucilla and Don Carlos sat practically silent through the meal. The food was good though not exceptional, but the wine flowed freely.

When it was over they all withdrew to the General's Sitting-Room and once again he sat on the sofa beside Joaquina, whom he called *La Gloriosa,* talking to her intimately.

"You must love *La Gloriosa* as I love her," he said to Lucilla and Don Carlos.

"Just as I love you, *Mi Glorioso,*" Joaquina interposed.

The General kissed her hand.

"You live in my heart, my sweet angel."

At last, because Lucilla felt that she and Don Carlos were intrusive, she rose to her feet.

"Will Your Excellency forgive me if I go to bed early?" she asked. "I have been travelling for eight days and I am very tired."

"But of course!" the General replied. "And once again, Miss Cunningham, let me thank you for your courage in undertaking such a hazardous journey in order to save my most valued colleague."

"I am only so glad that I arrived in time," Lucilla said.

She curtseyed and as she moved towards the door followed by Don Carlos, she realised that the General had already returned to the sofa and was once again flirting with the pretty *Señorita*.

Lucilla walked down the empty and quiet passages towards her own room.

Only when she reached the door did she turn to look up at Don Carlos, and found herself feeling suddenly breathless because he was so close to her.

She had a longing for him to kiss her again and hold her in his arms as he had done once before.

She wanted as she had never before wanted anything in her whole life to feel again the touch of his lips on hers.

But she felt rather than saw that he was reserved and withdrawn into himself as he had been in his portrait.

"I will arrange for you to leave tomorrow," he said in what she thought was a hard voice. "But as you are tired after travelling for so long, it will be a short day and you need not leave here until noon."

There was silence, then Lucilla said:

"I must . . . leave so . . . soon?"

She did not know really why she asked the question. It seemed to come from her lips without her considering what she was saying.

"I know your father must be worried about you," Don Carlos replied quietly.

She looked up at him and said:

"I should . . . not have . . . come here."

"I have already said it was very brave of you. You have saved me as you planned to do."

"That is all that matters," Lucilla said with a little sigh.

It was true, she thought; however angry her father might be, however damaged her reputation, nothing was of any consequence except that Don Carlos was safe, at any rate for the moment, from the intrigues and machinations of the Spaniards.

She made no movement to open the door and after a moment Don Carlos said:

"I think perhaps you were shocked tonight that the General seemed so interested in *Señorita* Joaquina."

"I was," Lucilla admitted frankly, "because I thought—in fact all Quito thought—that he loved . . . *Señora* Sáenz."

"When the General lost his wife," Don Carlos explained, "he vowed never to marry again. Women mean a lot to him, but like most men he has no wish to be tied down."

He paused and there was a faint smile on his lips as he added: —

"Manuela Sáenz is very possessive, very demanding."

"I think I . . . understand," Lucilla said hesitatingly.

"Every man has his Achilles' heel," Don Carlos went on, "and the General, because of the way he is made, because of his temperament, cannot do without female companionship."

"That is what they were saying in Quito," Lucilla murmured. "In fact they said there were even women who rose into battle beside him."

"That is true, but that was their decision, not his. He is driven to work harder, more violently, and for longer hours, than any other man alive. When he does allow himself to rest, it must be with a woman."

Lucilla gave a little sigh.

The corridor in which they were standing opened onto the court-yard where the moon rising in the sky was throwing its silver light over the slanting roofs and the climbing shrubs. It looked mysterious and very lovely.

She turned and walked a little way towards it almost instinctively, as if its beauty gave her reassurance.

She heard Don Carlos follow her and after a moment she said:

"I realise since coming to South America how ... ignorant and perhaps ... stupid I have been about so ... many things. I have never before understood wars or the men who fought them ... the horrors that are perpetrated ... the suffering that ... ensues."

She drew in her breath as she went on:

"They have only been words in books ... descriptive scenes that I did not understand as I had not seen them myself."

"And now you have?"

"I realise that women are useless except in their own ... environment, and the sooner I go back to ... England, the ... better."

"It is not true that you are useless," Don Carlos continued. "You have saved my life not once but twice. If you had not been here I should now be dead. Is that not an achievement?"

"I suppose it is," Lucilla agreed. "At the same time, if I had not saved you, perhaps some other ... woman would have ... done so."

Even as she spoke she felt a stab of sheer jealousy run through her. She knew that when she was gone there would be many other women to tend to him as they did to the General, to look after him, to love him.

'Who could help loving him when he is so attractive, so irresistible?' she thought wildly.

She had a sudden impulse to fling herself into his arms, to beg him to kiss her just once again so that she would have something to remember in the years ahead when she would be without him.

It would cost him nothing, it would mean nothing; but for her it would be a memory she could treasure in her heart for the rest of her life.

She was tinglingly conscious of him close beside her. She had only to make one little movement and she could be closer still.

Then in a voice that seemed somehow cold and uninterested Don Carlos said:

"You should rest now, Lucilla. It will be a long road back to Quito although you can return more slowly than when you came. I will send some of our best men with you so that you will be safe and protected until you are with your family again."

"Thank . . . you."

Lucilla's voice seemed to come from a far distance.

Now because she knew he expected it of her she turned her back on the moonlight.

"Buenos noches," she said as she curtseyed.

"Good-night, Lucilla," Don Carlos replied in English. "Sleep well."

She reached the door of her bed-room, opened it, and felt she was walking away from him into utter oblivion.

She heard his footsteps move down the passage, then as tears blinded her eyes she turned towards her bed.

* * *

Lucilla awoke early but she deliberately did not rise.

Instead she lay looking at the sunshine percolating through the cracks in the shutters and only after lying for a long time in thought did she open the shutters themselves to look out on the sun-lit day.

Don Carlos had said she was to leave at noon, and she thought that since perhaps he was with his soldiers or in attendance on the General there would be no point in her wandering about hoping to find him.

She would merely be an encumbrance in a world of men who were busy preparing for war.

So, having opened her window to let in the sun,

she lay on her bed and thought of the man she loved and the hopelessness of her love.

She told herself again that when he had kissed her it was no more than an expression of gratitude.

Had he wished to kiss her for herself, it would have been so easy to do so last night when they were alone looking at the moonlight with no-one to disturb them.

"I love him!" Lucilla told herself miserably. "And after today I shall never see him again."

She knew the General had not only to fight the Spaniards who were gathering in the mountains, but he also had to conquer the whole of Peru.

Lucilla knew little about warfare, but she was quite certain that if the Government set up by San Martín had failed, then it would be easy for the Spaniards to recapture the Capital and re-establish their old supremacy over the whole country.

Whatever happened, Don Carlos would be fighting for the Patriots and this time wearing the green uniform of his true allegiance.

Of one thing she was quite certain—he did not want her; so, as she had said to him, the sooner she returned to England, the better.

There she could try to convince herself that this was all some wonderful dream which had no substance in reality.

Her love was an agony; the pain within her seemed to grow every moment as she thought of Don Carlos.

Lucilla at last rose restlessly to wash and dress herself once again in the riding-habit she had been lent by Manuela Sáenz.

She could not help thinking bitterly of how the *Señora* was working and striving in Quito for General Bolívar, while he was flirting with other women, apparently quite unconcerned with all she was doing on his behalf.

"Like all men, he does not wish to be tied."

She could hear Don Carlos's voice saying the words and thought he was warning her not to lay her heart at his feet.

She hoped he did not know that she loved him, though she thought he must guess that the reason she had come so eagerly to find him in Guayaquil was more than a mere sense of patriotism and admiration for the cause.

Because of her love, she was prepared to sacrifice everything, her reputation, her family, and her pride.

She arranged her hair carefully in the mirror but did not put on the gold-trimmed képi, carrying it in her hand as she went from her bed-room.

She found a servant and instructed him to take her clothes to be packed in the panniers on the horse that would be accompanying her on her return journey.

It was about a quarter-to-twelve when she walked out onto the patio which surrounded the court-yard.

As she reached it her heart leapt when she saw Don Carlos dismounting from a horse outside the arched doorway.

He came walking towards her, his spurs jingling like the sound of bells, and she thought how handsome he looked in his green uniform, with the insignia of a Colonel on his shoulders on the gold epaulettes which decorated them.

"Good-morning," he said gravely. "You are ready to leave, I see."

Lucilla nodded. She did not trust her voice not to crack if she spoke to him.

"I have spoken to the men who will accompany you and told them they are not to travel too fast," Don Carlos said. "You should really rest for several days before you undertake such a journey again, but the hotels in Guayaquil are hopelessly inadequate and you cannot continue to stay here."

"N-no . . . of course not," Lucilla managed to say, and thought her voice sounded small and very far away.

"I have asked the General to write a letter of explanation to your father, telling him how much he appreciates your action in coming here."

"That was . . . kind of you."

"Perhaps you would like something to drink, some coffee, before you leave?"

She had the feeling that he was anxious for her to go, and although she longed to stay, she answered quickly:

"No, I think I should be on my way."

"As you wish," he answered.

As he spoke there was a sudden clatter of horses' hoofs, the sound of a command ringing out in Spanish, and into the court-yard came a lone rider.

It appeared to be a man astride a fiery black stallion. But as the horse was drawn to a halt, Lucilla stared in astonishment as she saw that it was not a man, as she had supposed, but Manuela Sáenz riding astride.

A soldier ran forward to go to the horse's head, and as she dismounted Lucilla felt suddenly embarrassed that she should appear so masculine and indeed so immodest.

"Manuela!" Don Carlos ejaculated, and Lucilla knew he was as surprised as she was at the *Señora*'s sudden appearance.

"You are astonished to see me, Carlos?" Manuela Sáenz asked, pulling off her riding-glove and giving him her hand.

She smiled up at him and looked so lovely as she did so that Lucilla felt a pang of irrepressible jealousy.

No-one, she thought, could look more beautiful, more fascinating, than this Spanish woman with her alabaster skin, her full lips, and her swift, flashing smile.

"Where is the General?" Manuela asked. "I have good news for him."

"He is here!" a voice said behind Lucilla, and General Bolívar came onto the patio.

"Is it possible—really possible—that I am seeing you with my own eyes?" he asked. "I have been thinking of you, dreaming of you, my darling, and now you are here."

He spoke passionately and Lucilla stared at him, unable to believe that he should be saying such things after the way he had been flirting last night with Joaquina.

"I have broken every record in reaching you," Manuela answered, "but I did not come alone."

She paused as if for dramatic effect, then said:

"Sir John Cunningham came with me."

"Papa!"

Lucilla breathed the words between her lips, but neither the General nor Don Carlos spoke. They only waited for Manuela Sáenz to explain.

"I have bought his ship-load of weapons for you," she said to the General, "bought and paid for them, and Sir John is at this moment arranging for them to be brought ashore."

"It is impossible!" General Bolívar exclaimed. "How have you found the money?"

Manuela made a little sound of sheer triumph.

"With Spanish gold!"

"But how? How is it possible?" General Bolívar asked.

Manuela smiled. Then she said:

"Give me a drink, Simón. I think I deserve it, and before I tell you any more, I want to say how good it is to see you and how much I have missed you."

There was a caressing note in her voice, and in Spanish the words sounded not only passionate but full of the yearning which Lucilla knew must have possessed her ever since she had been left behind in Quito.

They all sat down on the chairs on the patio. The General ordered coffee and wine, then eagerly as if he could no longer contain his curiosity he asked:

"Tell me, Manuela. Tell me everything that has happened."

He was holding her hand in his as he spoke. Bending his head, he first pressed his lips to the back of it, then turned it over and kissed the palm.

Manuela's dark eyes were radiant with love, then the twinkle returned as she said:

"When Miss Cunningham had left me, I lay awake all night thinking how I could find the money for that cargo, and as dawn broke I knew the answer."

"What was it?" the General enquired.

"The Spanish Treasurer in the Presidency! At first I could not remember if he had escaped, been executed, or was in prison. Then I learnt from Sucre that he was awaiting trial, and I went to the prison."

"How did you knew he could help you?" Don Carlos asked.

"There has never been a Spanish Government which has not kept ready money in reserve for the moment when the President or the Ministers wish to return to Spain," Manuela answered, and went on:

"I suppose I had always known it at the back of my mind, but I had forgotten in the excitement of liberating Quito that what we found in the Presidential Palace would only be a quarter of what must be hidden elsewhere."

"I did actually suggest to Sucre that there might be more than we discovered," General Bolívar remarked.

"I offered the Treasurer his life and his freedom if he would tell me where the reserves of the President were hidden," Manuela said.

"You were so sure such reserves did exist!"

"As sure as if an angel of the Lord had spoken to me!"

"And he told you?" Don Carlos questioned.

"He prevaricated quite a lot, but finally I threatened him with a somewhat unpleasant manner of dying, and he capitulated."

"How much?"

The words came from General Bolívar like a pistol-shot and Lucilla noticed that his fingers tightened on Manuela's hand.

She paused for sheer theatrical effect. Then slowly, almost as if she savoured every word, she answered:

"Three hundred thousand *pesos!*"

The General gave a cry of delight.

"Sir John and I left almost immediately," Manuela Sáenz said.

"Incredible! Marvellous!" General Bolívar exclaimed. "We need those weapons. We need every one of them!"

"That is what I knew," Manuela answered, and now her voice was serious.

The servants arrived with the coffee and the wine and as they set it down on the low table in front of them Manuela turned to Don Carlos.

"When I reached the quay just now with Sir John,"

she said, "there was a man who had just come ashore
from one of the ships. He was looking for you, Carlos."

"Looking for me?" Don Carlos exclaimed.

"I naturally enquired as to his business before
telling him where you were."

"Naturally!" Don Carlos replied.

There was a slight twist to his lips as if he knew
that it was Manuela Sáenz's curiosity rather than her
anxiety for his safety which had prompted her en-
quiry.

"The man had come from Scotland to find you."

Lucilla saw Don Carlos stiffen and his eyes were
on Manuela's face as he waited for her to continue.

"Your mother is dead," Manuela said quietly, "and
although I cannot understand why, it seems you are
now the Earl of Strathcraig."

For a moment Don Carlos did not speak, but the
General said:

"I am sorry to hear that you have had a family
bereavement, Carlos."

Then as if her sympathy was overcome by her
curiosity, Manuela asked:

"How can you inherit a title through your mother's death? I do not understand."

"In Scotland a title can descend in the female
line," he replied. "My grandfather was the Earl of
Strathcraig, but he had no son and on his death my
mother became Chief of the Clan."

"And now that she is dead you are the Earl?"

"That is right," Don Carlos agreed.

Lucilla knew that he was upset and she longed to
express her sympathy and make him understand how
sorry she was. But somehow it was impossible to say
the words with the General and Manuela there.

She could only look at him, hoping he would
understand without her saying anything.

In the pause that followed there was the sound of
footsteps in the court-yard. Lucilla turned her head
and gave a little exclamation which was more of fear
than of surprise; for it was her father who was coming
towards them.

He seemed large and authoritative and she felt too there was something aggressive about him.

The General rose to his feet.

"Good-morning, Sir John!" he said. "May I tell you how glad I am that the business which we discussed together has come to a satisfactory conclusion."

Sir John bowed and took the General's hand.

Watching him, Lucilla could see that he was incensed, and she thought apprehensively that the reason must rest with herself.

She was not mistaken, for her father turned from the General to look at her and she saw by the expression in his eyes how angry he was.

"So you are here, Lucilla!" he said harshly. *"Señora* Sáenz told me this is where I would find you. I shall have plenty to say about your behaviour on our return journey to Quito."

He looked at her, taking in the military cut of her jacket, and his eyes rested for a moment on the képi which she still held in her hand.

"I have brought some luggage for you with me, and you will kindly change out of those ridiculous garments into your own."

"Yes . . . Papa."

Lucilla's voice was weak and faint. As usual, her father deflated her to the point where she felt small and insignificant, and she was also afraid as she always was when he was angry with her.

She would have moved away, but Don Carlos came from behind the coffee-table to stand at her father's side.

"Your daughter, Sir John," he said, and he spoke in English, "came here to save my life. It was amazingly courageous of her, and both I and the General will tell you that her action may also have saved the Patriot Army from suffering a disastrous defeat."

Sir John inclined his head, but Lucilla knew he was not at all impressed and was not concerning himself with anything but her own behaviour.

"Miss Cunningham and I have known each other for some time," Don Carlos continued, "and I therefore have the very great honour, Sir John, in asking for her hand in marriage!"

If he had thrown a bomb into the midst of them, Don Carlos could not have caused a greater sensation than by his quiet words.

Lucilla drew in her breath and felt she was turned to stone, while she saw the incredulous surprise on the faces of Manuela Sáenz and the General.

The General recovered first.

"My dear Carlos," he exclaimed, "I have heard nothing that could please me more. Let me congratulate you, and you, too, Sir John, for you have found yourself the finest son-in-law that any man could ask."

The General reached forward to shake Don Carlos's hand, then Sir John's.

A mischievous smile lit up Manuela Sáenz's lovely face.

"I too must congratulate you, Carlos," she said. "It is a surprise, a very great surprise, but of course we all know that love wins the last battle."

There was something mocking in her tone and Lucilla felt uncomfortable, as she had done when she realised that Manuela Sáenz had sent her to Guayaquil in person when she could quite easily have sent a messenger.

"We must talk further about this," Sir John said pompously and without enthusiasm.

"You have not yet heard, Sir John," Manuela said, "that Carlos has just learnt that he is now the Earl of Strathcraig."

Sir John stared at her, then at Don Carlos, in bewilderment.

"The Earl of Strathcraig?" he repeated uncomprehendingly.

"My mother is dead," Don Carlos said quietly.

"I have met the old Earl," Sir John said.

"My grandfather!"

There was a silence while Lucilla knew her father was slowly absorbing with a businesslike efficiency the information he had been given.

He was considering whether to give his consent to her marriage or to oppose it.

But she knew without being told that he would agree, simply because now Don Carlos was not a Spaniard and a foreigner, but a Scotsman and an Earl.

He was a fellow-countryman whom he would respect and with whom he would be only too pleased for his family to be allied.

Then Lucilla suddenly realised that whatever her father said, whatever congratulations the General and Manuela might offer, she could not marry Don Carlos.

She knew only too well that as a man of honour he had offered for her simply because she had stayed the night in the *hacienda* without a Chaperon.

She had forced herself upon him and she had not fully realised how outrageous her behaviour would seem in the eyes of her father and indeed to anyone else who heard of it.

Aloud she said in a voice that trembled:

"I will go and . . . change . . . Papa."

She moved away towards her bed-room without looking at Don Carlos.

When she reached it she sat down in front of the mirror and put her hands up to her cheeks.

It did not seem possible that Don Carlos had asked for her hand in marriage when she was on the very point of saying good-bye to him forever.

Then she told herself that because he was chivalrous, because he was gallant as perhaps another man might not have been, she could not take advantage of him.

She could think of nothing nearer Heaven than to be married to him, to belong to him. Even if he never really loved her, she felt as if her own love was so great, so overwhelming, that it would be enough for them both.

Then she knew she was deceiving herself. He did not love her and marriage without love was unthinkable.

There was a knock at the door and when she said, "Come in," two soldiers entered, carrying her trunk and a bonnet-box which her father had brought with him from Quito.

They set them down on the floor and when they

had gone Lucilla forced herself to open the trunk and take out a travelling-gown of blue silk and a mantel of the same colour.

There was a small bonnet to wear with them, and she took off the riding-habit which Manuela Sáenz had lent her and changed into her own clothes.

She felt as if she had finally set aside all that was adventurous and novel in her character and had gone back to what she had been before leaving England.

She had begun to change, she thought, from the moment she had walked into the Pavilion and found Don Carlos standing there before he fell to the ground, telling her he was dead.

That was the moment when she developed a new personality, a new individuality. She had decided, without fear of the consequences, to hide him and nurse him back to health, and she knew now that she had fallen more in love with him every moment they were together.

"But what have I to offer him?" she asked herself. "He has done so much! He has lived an exciting life, a life of danger, a life of great bravery. When he marries, it should be to someone like Manuela Sáenz."

She sighed and it was not only a sigh for herself but also for Manuela.

The General had been, it was obvious, intensely pleased to see her, but once she left him again there would be other women.

That was not real love, Lucilla thought, not the sort of love that she felt for Don Carlos; for there would never, she knew, be another man in her life. Even if she never, from this moment, saw him again, he would still be the only man who mattered.

But with men it was different. She faced the fact and was not prepared to condemn the General, even though her heart bled for Manuela.

When she was dressed, thinking as she did so both of Manuela and of herself, she knew that only a woman would understand what she was feeling at the moment.

Picking up the green habit, she put it over her arm and went to the door. A servant was passing down the corridor.

"Can you tell me which room *Señora* Sáenz is using?" she asked.

"I have just taken her things there, *Señorita*," the servant answered. "It is the third door in the next passage to the right."

"Thank you," Lucilla answered.

She walked there quickly, knocked on the door, and heard Manuela's voice tell her to enter.

She half-turned from the dressing-table as Lucilla entered, and exclaimed:

"Oh, it is you, Miss Cunningham!"

Lucilla shut the door behind her.

"I have brought back the habit you so kindly lent me," she said, putting it down on a chair.

"It was a pleasure!" Manuela Sáenz replied. "But I am afraid your father is very angry with you. He ranted and roared all the way from Quito to Guayaquil. But now you are to be the wife of a Scottish Earl, I dare say he will forgive you."

"*Señora,* I need your help."

"My help?"

Manuela turned completely round from the dressing-table.

She had taken off her military coat, and sitting in her riding-breeches, wearing polished boots and a white lawn shirt, she was like a slender boy until one looked at her beautiful face with its mischievous eyes.

"Now what is wrong?" she enquired.

Lucilla felt for words.

"Don Carlos does not really wish to marry me," she said. "He has asked me only because he thought in coming here I compromised myself."

"But he has asked you," Manuela said. "That is something he has never asked of any other woman, I can assure you!"

"That is not the point," Lucilla said. "He does not love me, so I . . . cannot marry him."

"Are you prepared to tell him so? What will your father say?"

"That is why I want you to help me," Lucilla said. "Please, *Señora,* you have so much power, so much authority. Can you arrange for me to leave immediately for England? There must be a ship in which I can travel as a passenger."

"Is that what you really want?" Manuela Sáenz asked. "Have you considered how attractive Carlos is? And how eligible, now that he has come into a title?"

"None of that is important," Lucilla replied.

"Most women marry without love," Manuela said. "I did!"

Lucilla did not reply, but her silence must have made the inference obvious, for Manuela laughed.

"All right. There is no need to put what you are thinking into words," she said. "At the same time, you are English and far more respectable than I am ever likely to be. You have lost your good name by coming here to help Carlos. It is only right and just that he should look after you for the rest of your life."

"No, no!" Lucilla said passionately. "I will not marry him for that reason."

"Do you love him?"

"Yes, I love him. I love him too much to spoil his life in such a ridiculous manner!"

Her words seemed to ring out. Then she said in a quiet tone:

"Please help me, *Señora*. If I can get back to England, I can stay with my cousin there until my father returns. He finds me useful as a housekeeper, so he will forget his anger once we are home again."

"I have a feeling that your father will be extremely angry if you refuse such an advantageous marriage."

"There is nothing else I can do," Lucilla said. "You must see that! Don Carlos does not really want me. I mean nothing to him."

"Don Carlos is a strange man," Manuela said reflectively. "Women do not matter in his life as they do in the General's."

She went on almost as if she was speaking to herself:

"There have been women, of course, because he is a man; but his heart has never been involved, although many women have offered him theirs."

Lucilla was sure that was the truth. How could anybody be with Don Carlos, she thought, and not love him? He was so attractive, so much everything a man should be.

And yet, if what Manuela said was true and he had never been in love, he must have an ideal of what the woman he would love would be like.

It was quite obvious it was not she.

Suppose she married him, she thought to herself, and then he found his ideal woman and was not free to marry her?

Whatever she was suffering now would be nothing compared to the agony she would feel in such circumstances.

Aloud she said:

"I must get . . . away."

Manuela had been watching her while she lit a cigar.

Now she rose with it between her lips and walked to the window.

"There is a ship in the harbour which will doubtless be sailing at dawn," she said. "Are you really prepared for me to arrange your passage to England?"

"Yes, please," Lucilla said. "Please . . . please do that."

"Very well," Manuela replied. "I will persuade your father to stay and superintend the complete unloading of his ship. He intended, I know, that you should both return to Quito today, but I will tell him it is impossible and he must be here."

"It is very kind of you," Lucilla murmured.

"I will arrange for your luggage to be taken from your room when we are at dinner," Manuela went on. "You can retire to bed early and a carriage will be waiting for you."

"I am grateful . . . very grateful."

"Quite frankly, I think you are a fool," she replied. "You have managed to make Carlos say the words no other woman has ever heard. He has offered you marriage, and although I do not know Scotland I imagine he has a position of importance there. Change your mind, Miss Cunningham!"

Lucilla shook her head.

"No . . . please . . . I just want to go home . . .

alone. Perhaps when I have gone you will tell Papa why I had no wish to marry in ... such circumstances. Please tell ... Don Carlos too."

"Very well," Manuela agreed briskly. "If you have made up your mind, there is no point in discussing it further. Go to your room and take off your travelling things and put on something cool. I will talk with your father as soon as I am changed."

"I am very grateful ... more grateful than I can possibly say," Lucilla cried.

"I do not want your gratitude," Manuela replied. "All that pleases me is that your father brought those magnificent weapons to South America and I have managed to make the Spaniards pay for them!"

Lucilla went back to her own room and changed, as Manuela had suggested, into a thin gown.

She took a long time over it, knowing she had no wish to see her father before Manuela had persuaded him to change his plans.

When finally she came from her bed-room it was to discover that her father, Manuela Sáenz, and the General had gone to the quay to watch the unloading of the cargo.

There was no sign of Don Carlos either, and when it was luncheon-time only Charles Sowerby appeared with Daniel O'Leary, whom Lucilla had not met since the Victory Ball in Quito.

They did not volunteer information as to where Don Carlos had gone, and Lucilla did not like to ask too many questions.

While they ate, Daniel O'Leary talked all the time of the dramatic meeting that had taken place between the General and San Martín.

"I am keeping records," he told Lucilla, "of everything the General does, because one day it will make history."

"Better you than me," Charles Sowerby said. "If there is one thing I hate, it is having to write reports, and it seems to me you are setting yourself a task that will grow more wearisome year by year."

"I am not thinking of myself," Daniel O'Leary replied, "though doubtless you are right. What is impor-

tant is that the world should know the greatness of
Simón Bolívar, and who will know it if we who love
him do not write his story as it should be written?"

"I think it is very wonderful of you," Lucilla said.

"Thank you," Daniel O'Leary answered. "As
Charles says, it is doubtless going to be a wearisome
task."

After luncheon, because there was nothing else to
do and it was time for *siesta,* Lucilla went to her own
room to lie down.

She was half-asleep when Manuela came in.

She shut the door behind her and said in a low
voice:

"It is arranged, but you must be careful not to
let your father be suspicious."

"No, of course not," Lucilla said, sitting up in bed.

"He and Don Carlos are arranging your marriage
as soon as your sister, Catherine, can get here from
Quito, and then you can all travel to Scotland in your
own ship."

Just for a moment Lucilla felt the room swim
round her.

Could anything be more wonderful, she thought,
than to be in Scotland, which she loved, with Don Carlos?

She said nothing, and Manuela, sitting down on the
side of the bed, said:

"It is strange, I never realised that Don Carlos's
mother was Scottish. Apparently she quarrelled with his
father, who, of course, came from one of the finest
and noblest aristocratic families in the New World,
and she went back to her own people."

"So Don Carlos was brought up by his father,"
Lucilla said.

"Yes, both in Venezuela, where his father lived,
and at the Court of Spain at Madrid."

Manuela smiled as she went on:

"Heaven knows how he ever got to know Simón
Bolívar. He must have been very young when the General started his fight for independence. But I understand Don Carlos offered him his services."

"And of course the General accepted them," Lucilla said with a smile.

"Simón tells me now that he realised how useful Carlos could be if he remained with the Spaniards with whom he had been brought up and communicated secretly with the Patriots."

"It was a heavy burden to place on someone so young," Lucilla said quietly.

"Simón knew that. But he was well aware how intelligent Carlos was, and all through the years his assistance to the Liberator has grown and been of inestimable value."

Lucilla felt herself glow with pride.

"He is very wonderful!" she said softly.

"But you still intend not to marry him?" Manuela asked.

"Yes . . . and I have told you why," Lucilla answered.

"Very well," Manuela said. "Everything is arranged. Retire to bed as soon as dinner is over. A closed carriage will be outside a side-door of the *hacienda*."

"Thank you," Lucilla said. "Thank you . . . very much."

Chapter Seven

Lucilla went to her bed-room to pick up her fur-lined cloak, which was lying on the bed.

She thought it would be too hot to wear it. At the same time, it was the only thing of hers that had not been packed and taken away.

She glanced round, feeling that she was closing the door once and for all on a chapter in her life that that had been more wonderful, and yet more heart-breaking, than anything else she had ever known.

All through dinner it had been impossible to look at Don Carlos as he sat opposite her on the other side of the table.

She kept her eyes lowered, finding it hard to eat anything, but pretending that she was for the sake of appearances.

Fortunately, the General was in good spirits and made up for any deficiencies on the part of his guests.

He had invited Charles Sowerby and Daniel O'Leary to dinner and they encouraged him to reminisce on the battles in which they had taken part and the times when they had defeated the Spaniards against overwhelming odds.

Lucilla knew that the General was talking really to Manuela, showing off, impressing her, making her appreciate that his reputation as a hero had every foundation in fact.

Lucilla actually heard little of what he said and what she did hear made no sense. All she could think of was that this was the last time she would see Don Carlos, and how much she loved him.

They rose from the table and while the men sauntered out onto the patio where coffee was waiting for them, Lucilla had slipped away down the passages to her own bed-room.

Now as she picked up her cloak, the door opened and Manuela Sáenz came in.

Lucilla had an apprehensive feeling that perhaps the plans had been changed at the last moment.

"I merely came to ask you if you are quite intent on making this useless gesture," Manuela Sáenz asked.

She was looking exceedingly lovely in a very décolleté gown which was of a deep emerald green and made her look even more seductive than usual.

If anything, it strengthened Lucilla's resolve to leave.

How could she compete with anyone like Manuela? She was quite certain that in the past the women who had loved Don Carlos had looked like her and been self-assured, confident of their charms, and sophisticated as she could never hope to be in a million years.

"Yes . . . I must go," Lucilla murmured.

Manuela walked to the open window. The sun had just sunk in a blaze of glory, and now that it was growing dark, there was the quietness which always seemed to hang over the world at dusk.

"I thought you had more courage," Manuela said.

Lucilla looked at her questioningly as she went on:

"To fight for what you want, because I can assure you nothing is really unobtainable. It is always possible to win in the end."

Lucilla knew she was speaking for herself and as she did not answer Manuela continued:

"The General loves me at the moment as he has loved many women before. But I want more from him than the fire which makes us physically indispensable to each other."

"More?" Lucilla asked, not understanding what she was saying.

"I want something that no other woman has ever had before," Manuela said in a low voice. "I want the very essence of him, his spirit, his soul, and I swear to you that however long it takes, one day he will be completely mine. Then I shall know I have fulfilled my destiny."

She spoke almost as if she was making a vow.

"You are running away," she went on, "but I shall go on fighting: Simón Bolívar will then not be the victor but a man conquered by a love so overwhelming, so great, that he himself does not know he is capable of it."

Because Lucilla felt Manuela was speaking intimately in a manner that made her seem feminine and vulnerable, she did not reply.

She felt as if she were overhearing a conversation that was not intended for her ears.

Then with a quick change of mood that was characteristic of her, Manuela turned round from the window.

"Hurry, child!" she exclaimed. "If you intend to leave, you must do so at once. It is all arranged! A boat will take you to the *Saucy Kate,* which is anchored in the harbour. It is a cargo-ship carrying coffee to England. It may not be very comfortable, but it will serve your purpose."

"I am very grateful?" Lucilla said. "Can I pay you for my passage?"

"You can do so on board. I have arranged it," Manuela replied. "All you have to do is pay for the carriage and tip the men who will row you to the ship."

Lucilla put her heavy cloak over her shoulders. It covered the white gown she had worn for dinner and she did not wish to be seen as she left the *hacienda.*

She would take it off, she thought, as soon as she reached the carriage.

"Good-bye, *Señora,*" she said, "and thank you again."

"*Adiós,*" Manuela replied lightly.

She watched Lucilla move down the passage, and closing the bed-room door, she walked back to the patio to join General Bolívar.

The carriage which was waiting for Lucilla was

old and rickety and just what one might expect, she thought, of a hired vehicle in Guayaquil.

There was only one tired horse to draw it and it moved very slowly over the bumpy road. Even so she was thrown from side to side in an uncomfortable fashion.

The carriage smelt of age, dust, and hay. She opened the window to feel the cool of the night air on her cheeks, trying to look out for the last time at the land which she had found so beautiful.

The darkness spreading over the sky hid the mountains and the stars had not yet appeared to illuminate the undulating ground over which they were moving.

First there was the brightness of the lanterns which the soldiers used in their tents or outside the rough shelters they had erected round the *hacienda*.

But soon there was only darkness and the two candlelights on the carriage, until in the distance Lucilla could see the bright lights of the houses of Guayaquil and beyond them those of the ships in the harbour.

It seemed to her to take a very long time before they reached the houses on stilts and turned down the dusty, dirty road which led to the quay.

They passed the Churches, the saw-mill, and a rope factory which had been pointed out to Lucilla when she arrived, where the Indians worked the tough-fibered cabuya into thick plaited ropes for the ships.

Then they had reached the quay and she knew that this was where she was leaving the soil of South America forever.

The cab-driver got down with some difficulty from his seat and opened the door.

Lucilla stepped out, feeling the wind from the sea in her hair, and pulled her cloak closely round her because she thought she would look strange embarking in a row-boat.

It was waiting a little ahead at the beginning of the jetty and she walked towards it followed by the cab-driver carrying her trunk and complaining beneath his breath at its weight.

"*Señorita* Cunningham?" a man asked.

She stood looking at the two oarsmen sitting in the boat.

Her name was pronounced in a strange way, but the men were undoubtedly waiting for her. Then, having helped Lucilla aboard, they took her trunk from the driver and set it down in the boat.

He returned to the carriage for her hat-box, and rocking on the water Lucilla looked round the harbour at dozens of anchored ships, their port and starboard lights reflected red and green on the sea below them.

She wondered which was the *Saucy Kate* and hoped it would not be too small a vessel.

It had been rough as they crossed the Atlantic in her father's ship, which was comparatively large and well-built.

Although Lucilla had not been sea-sick, because she was a good sailor, the continual pitching, tossing, and rolling had been extremely uncomfortable, and she had been frightened of breaking a leg or an arm.

The cab-man brought her hat-box and she paid him for conveying her from the *hacienda,* knowing the sum he asked was an exorbitant one.

He did not thank her for what she gave him even though she included a tip, but walked away in a surly manner which was very unlike the charm and friendliness of the people of Quito.

The oarsmen pushed off from the jetty and began to row slowly and without exerting themselves into the centre of the great harbour.

Because she dared not think of Don Carlos, feeling that if she did so she would begin to cry, Lucilla tried to think of the pirates for whom Guayaquil had become a magnet in the sixteenth century.

Francis Drake had captured a treasure-ship here and had divided amongst his freebooters a huge amount of silver plate. After him there had been many famous pirates, including one who in a mad fury caught the town unprepared and sacked and burned it.

She tried to keep her mind on the history she had read but all she could think about was her own.

"I love him! I love him!" she whispered to herself, and knew that because he meant so much to her she could not accept his chivalry but must creep away in the darkness out of his life and leave him free to find a woman he would love as much as she loved him.

Because she was fighting against her tears, Lucilla found it impossible to continue to look round her. Instead, she bent her head and clasped her fingers tightly together in an effort at self-control.

All she could think of was Don Carlos sitting talking on the patio with her father, planning their marriage and not realising until tomorrow morning that she was already on her way back to England—alone.

"We are here, *Señorita!*" one of the oarsmen said.

Looking up, Lucilla realised they were alongside a vessel which towered above them, and there was a rope-ladder up which she was to climb to reach the deck.

She had climbed rope-ladders before, and once the men had assisted her to get her feet firmly on the first rungs, she climbed up without difficulty despite the heaviness of her fur-lined cape.

There was an Officer waiting to assist her on deck. She saw that he looked smarter than might have been expected on a cargo-ship and she thought that perhaps after all she would not be as uncomfortable as she had feared.

The ship too seemed very large and her fears of the ocean abated.

"Will you come this way, Miss?" the Officer asked.

He spoke in English, and she followed him obediently down a companionway. They walked along a narrow passage towards the stern.

The ship certainly, Lucilla thought again, seemed much larger than she had expected the *Saucy Kate* would be, and she told herself the cargo must be a valuable one, so that the Captain would therefore make every effort to ensure that they arrived in safety.

Her father had always been very scathing about cargo-ships, which was why he was prepared to carry his own merchandise rather than rely on vessels he could charter.

'Papa would be surprised at this ship!' Lucilla thought to herself.

The Officer opened a door and stood back for her to enter.

She had expected a small cabin, but to her surprise she realised that she was entering a very large one. Then she saw two men standing at the far end of it, and felt as if she had been turned to stone.

It was Don Carlos who stood there.

Don Carlos, looking tall and authoritative and so overwhelmingly handsome that she wanted to forget everything else and run to him and tell him how glad she was to see him.

Instead, it was impossible to move and almost impossible to breathe.

She heard the cabin door close behind her, then he was at her side, taking her hand in his.

She felt herself thrill at the touch of his fingers, and he said very quietly:

"Father Pablo is here to marry us. We have not much time, since the battleship is due to sail on the turn of the tide."

"B-but . . . I . . . I . . ." Lucilla began to stammer.

Then with his eyes on hers he smiled down at her and the words died on her lips.

"I know," he said so quietly that only she could hear, "but as I have arranged that we shall share a cabin on our way home, you really must think of my reputation!"

She wanted to answer him, but somehow it was impossible to think of anything but the laughter in his eyes. He raised her hand and kissed it.

"Come," he said, "there will be plenty of time later for all the explanations."

He drew her a step forward, and then as if he saw that her cloak was heavy and cumbersome he lifted it from her shoulders and laid it down on a chair.

Almost before Lucilla realised it was happening, they were standing in front of the Priest and he was saying the words of the Marriage Service in Latin.

It only took a very short time, but for Lucilla it was as if the Heavens opened and a chorus of angels sang round them. For the first time she heard Don Carlos's name spoken in English.

"Charles Anthony Francis."

He repeated the words slowly as if he wanted her to hear them, but her own response was in such a small and frightened tone that she thought he could not have heard it.

They knelt, their hands were joined together, and the Priest blessed them.

When they rose, Don Carlos once again raised Lucilla's hand to his lips. Then he escorted the Priest from the cabin and for the first time she could look round her.

She realised immediately that they were in the Captain's cabin and she knew that in the time-honoured tradition it was the most important accommodation in a warship.

It was spacious and comfortable and there was a large box-bed built against one wall, draped with curtains that could be pulled in the daytime or at night if the occupants needed privacy.

Lucilla blushed and sat down suddenly on a chair, feeling, though the ship was not yet moving, as if it were turning turtle and the whole world she knew was rocking crazily round her.

It could not have happened! It could not be true that she was married to Don Carlos after trying so hard to escape from him!

She knew the warship was one of those under the command of Admiral Lord Cochrane.

She remembered that Admiral Lord Cochrane was a Scotsman, and thought it must have been a matter of blood calling to blood which was enabling them to sail home so comfortably.

A few moments later Don Carlos came back into the cabin. With her heart beating frantically, Lucilla rose to her feet to stand trembling as, having shut the door, he stood looking at her.

"Why did you run away?" he asked. His voice was deep and, she thought, perhaps a little angry.

"I . . . I had to . . . . go," she replied, "you should not have . . . stopped me."

"Why not?"

"B-because I did not intend to . . . marry you."

"Why not?" he asked again.

"Because . . . it was . . . wrong . . . you did not . . . really wish to be . . . married."

He moved towards her, and, because she was frightened of her own feelings and the frantic fluttering of her heart, she turned away from him to look out one of the port-holes.

She felt him stand behind her, and, knowing he was so near, she longed to turn round and hide her face against his shoulder.

Even now she could not believe he had stopped her from trying to escape, and they were married.

"How . . . did you know when . . . I had . . . left the *hacienda* . . . and where I had gone?" she asked a little incoherently.

He gave a laugh that sounded young and happy.

"You forget I have been a spy for a great number of years, and a very good one."

"Then . . . Manuela did not . . . tell you?"

"Manuela acted almost as convincingly as you did," he answered.

"Then how did you . . . know?"

"I sensed what you were feeling, for I have been with you too long, Lucilla, not to be aware when you are worried and perturbed. I know a great number of other things as well."

There was a note in his voice as he spoke which made her feel stranger than she had ever before felt in her whole life, and at the same time so intensely excited that it was like a pain.

"I want you to tell me," Don Carlos said very quietly, "what you felt when I kissed you good-bye in the little Pavilion."

"It was . . . wonderful!" Lucilla answered without pausing to think. "The most wonderful . . . perfect . . . thing that ever . . . happened to me. I knew it meant . . . nothing to you . . . but it was something I can never forget . . . something I shall . . . treasure all my life!"

"That is exactly what I felt."

Lucilla was so surprised that she turned round to

look at him, her eyes very wide. At the expression in his eyes she drew in her breath.

"Why should you think it meant nothing to me, my darling?" Don Carlos asked. "I knew then that you loved me as I loved you."

"You . . . loved me?" Lucilla could hardly breathe the words.

"I loved you from the very first moment I saw you, and when you nursed me and read to me I knew you were everything I ever dreamt a woman should be."

"Why did you not . . . tell me?"

She thought of the agony she had passed through, trying to keep him from knowing of her love, telling herself again and again that she was so unimportant and so insignificant that she could mean nothing to him.

"I had nothing to offer you," he replied. "I had given up my father's fortune, and in the years I was working for the Patriots I took as little as I possibly could from the Spaniards."

She thought it was like him to be so honourable, if only to himself.

"How could I ask you to share my life?" he went on. "A life not only of hardship and privation, but of desperate physical danger."

He paused before he continued:

"At any moment, any day or night, someone might have betrayed me and I would have been tortured and killed, not quickly, but slowly. Do you think I would really let you risk that?"

"I would not have cared . . . as long as I could be with . . . you," Lucilla whispered.

"That is what I wanted you to say," Don Carlos answered, "and I knew when I kissed you that if I had asked you to come with me you would have done so."

He smiled very tenderly as he asked:

"Is that not true?"

"You know I would have gone . . . anywhere . . . to the ends of the world with . . . you," Lucilla answered, and there was a passionate note in her voice.

"I can hardly believe it is true," Don Carlos said

almost as if he spoke to himself, "but now I have something to offer you instead of a life of fear. I am only afraid, my adventurous little wife, that you may find it very dull."

"You are the one who may find that," Lucilla answered. "Will you really be content to live quietly in Scotland and . . . with me?"

There was a little sob in the last words and she knew that this was a very real fear . . . that he would find her dull and insignificant as her father had always done.

Very slowly he put his arms round her and drew her close against him, then he turned her face up to his.

"There is so much for us to discover about each other," he said, "and I promise you, my precious, it will be the most exciting thing I have ever done in my life."

Then his lips were on hers and she felt the wonder and the glory that she had felt before sweep over her like a wave from the sea.

For a moment it was so intense, so glorious, that she was afraid. Then she pressed herself against him, feeling that the closeness and the wonder of him was even more ecstatic than it had been before.

Now she belonged to him, she was his, and she knew she had never before known the beauty and the wonder of living until his lips touched hers.

Once again there were the mountains, the flowers, and the sunshine in his kiss, but now it was more personal, more intimate, as their love drew them close, each to each, together with something else which as Manuela had described to her was deeper and more intense than love itself.

'It is not only our hearts but our souls that are touching each other,' Lucilla thought.

Then the intensity of her feelings made it impossible to think, but only to feel. . . .

It seemed to her a long time later before Don Carlos raised his head to look down at her face, radiant in the light from the lanterns, her eyes shining like the stars that were coming out in the sky.

"I love . . . you!" she whispered brokenly.

Then because she was shy she hid her face against his shoulder.

He kissed her hair.

"And I love you, my darling! You are mine, and I shall make quite sure that you never try to escape from me again."

"It was an . . . agony to leave . . . you," Lucilla murmured.

"And an agony for me when I learnt what you intended," he said. "At first I could not believe it. I thought you must know how much I wanted you."

"You . . . never told me . . . so."

He gave a sigh.

"You have no idea how much self-control I exerted not to kiss you last night when we stood on the patio looking at the moonlight."

"I wanted you to . . . kiss me . . . I longed for you to . . . do . . . so."

"I knew that," he answered, "but I did not think it was fair when I was sending you back to your father —to safety and security. I thought it would be harder for both of us if I held you like this and kissed you as I wanted to."

Lucilla raised her head again.

"Kiss me now . . . please kiss me," she said. "I still cannot believe . . . that I am not . . . dreaming."

"I will make you believe you are awake," he answered, "but first, my beautiful darling, I will tell the sailors to bring your luggage in here. Then no-one will disturb us for the rest of the night."

There was a passion in his voice that made Lucilla blush again.

"Suppose," she whispered, "I disappoint you and I am not . . . after all, your . . . ideal woman . . . the woman you have been looking for for . . . so long."

"How do you know I have been looking for someone like that?" Don Carlos asked.

"Manuela told me you had never asked anyone to marry you."

"That is true, although I have no idea how Manuela knows such things."

Lucilla laughed.

"I think, like you, she knows or senses things about people which they do not even know themselves."

"Such as?" Don Carlos prompted.

"She told me she is fighting a battle with General Bolívar to make him love her as he has never loved a woman before and never will again."

Don Carlos smiled.

"It is a naked battle when two people are alone and the trappings of pomp and glory are laid aside for love."

He was saying exactly what she herself had thought, and as she looked at him in surprise he said very quietly:

"That is a battle I shall fight with you, my darling, because I not only wish to possess your beautiful body and your soft, entrancing lips, I want the thoughts you think, the beat of your heart, and that spiritual force within you which you call your soul."

"It is yours! All yours!" Lucilla cried. "There is no need for a battle. You have won already!"

"I must make sure of that."

He pulled her closer to him and kissed her passionately and demandingly as if he would force from her what he needed and make it his.

And as he kissed her, as his lips pressed themselves against her mouth, her eyes, her cheeks, and the softness of her neck, Lucilla felt a fire rise within her, ignited, she knew, by the fire in him.

"I love . . . you . . ." she tried to say, but her voice was deep and passionate and seemed almost to be strangled in her throat.

"You are mine!" Don Carlos cried. "Mine completely and absolutely."

He kissed her again until she felt the world disappear and once again they were on a secret island of their own surrounded by a boundless sea.

It was what she had felt when she was with him in the little Pavilion; but now it was more real, more wonderful, more intense.

Ever since she had known him she had changed and become alive to new possibilities within herself.

Now she knew she could never go back to what she was before, because she had been reborn! Reborn to a new life, and above all to love.

It was a love that was perfect, and Divine, a love that was not only of the body but of the soul and the spirit.

"I love you! Oh, Carlos ... I love you with ... all of me!" she whispered.

He took the last words from her lips, saying fiercely:

"You are mine, my beautiful, adorable wife. now and for all eternity!"

ABOUT THE AUTHOR

BARBARA CARTLAND, the celebrated romantic author, historian, playwright, lecturer, political speaker and television personality, has now written over 150 books. Miss Cartland has had a number of historical books published and several biographical ones, including that of her brother, Major Ronald Cartland, who was the first Member of Parliament to be killed in the War. This book had a Foreword by Sir Winston Churchill.

In private life, Barbara Cartland, who is a Dame of the Order of St. John of Jerusalem, has fought for better conditions and salaries for Midwives and Nurses. As President of the Royal College of Midwives (Hertfordshire Branch), she has been invested with the first Badge of Office ever given in Great Britain, which was subscribed to by the Midwives themselves. She has also championed the cause for old people and founded the first Romany Gypsy Camp in the world.

Barbara Cartland is deeply interested in Vitamin Therapy and is President of the British National Association for Health.

Barbara Cartland

The world's bestselling author of romantic fiction.
Her stories are always captivating tales of intrigue,
adventure and love.

☐	A VERY NAUGHTY ANGEL	2107	$1.25
☐	CALL OF THE HEART	2140	$1.25
☐	AS EAGLES FLY	2147	$1.25
☐	THE TEARS OF LOVE	2148	$1.25
☐	THE DEVIL IN LOVE	2149	$1.25
☐	THE ELUSIVE EARL	2436	$1.25
☐	A DREAM FROM THE NIGHT	2972	$1.25
☐	THE BORED BRIDEGROOM	6381	$1.25
☐	THE PENNILESS PEER	6387	$1.25
☐	THE LITTLE ADVENTURE	6428	$1.25
☐	LESSONS IN LOVE	6431	$1.25
☐	THE DARING DECEPTION	6435	$1.25
☐	CASTLE OF FEAR	8103	$1.25
☐	THE RUTHLESS RAKE	8240	$1.25
☐	THE DANGEROUS DANDY	8280	$1.25
☐	THE WICKED MARQUIS	8467	$1.25
☐	LOVE IS INNOCENT	8505	$1.25
☐	THE FRIGHTENED BRIDE	8780	$1.25
☐	THE FLAME IS LOVE	8887	$1.25